A LITTLE BIT OF PASSION

•

Beate Boeker

AVALON BOOKS
NEW YORK

Published by Avalon Books,
an imprint of Thomas Bouregy & Co., Inc.
160 Madison Avenue, New York, NY 10016

Library of Congress Cataloging-in-Publication Data

Boeker, Beate.
    A little bit of passion / Beate Boeker.
        p. cm.
    ISBN 978-0-8034-7650-9 (acid-free paper)   1. Women
skiers—Fiction.   2. Women booksellers—Fiction   3. Skis and
skiing—Teton Range (Wyo. and Idaho)—Fiction.   4. Bookstores—
New York (State)—Long Island—Fiction.   I. Title.
    PR9110.9.B64L58 2011
    823'.92—dc22
                                                            2010037159

PRINTED IN THE UNITED STATES OF AMERICA
ON ACID-FREE PAPER
BY RR DONNELLEY, BLOOMSBURG, PENNSYLVANIA

*To Margaret D. Elam, who taught me
how to make words sing*

Chapter One

Teton Mountain Range

Dear Leslie,

Do you remember the guy who made me think for the first time that I'm too old to teach skiing? I was so glad when he finished his course last year and took his turtle-y head elsewhere.

Well, he's back.

I greeted my new ten o'clock group this morning, and the instant I finished introducing myself, he sidled out from behind someone else's back and stared at me with his half-closed eyes. A shiver ran down my spine, and I'm sure I looked as if I had discovered a huge spider among the Easter eggs. He must have been hiding at the guesthouse this morning, or I would have been on my guard.

I turned my back on him as soon as I could, but I knew he continued to watch me, his head swiveling from left to right like a hundred-year-old turtle's. That image really fits, right down to the wrinkles all over the face and the folds in the neck. You can't imagine how stiffly I moved all at once, like a wooden doll, waiting for his first nasty comment.

1

I didn't have to wait long. Just as I showed them how to swing into an arc, he muttered in that penetrating voice of his, "Show me again how to swing that hip, baby. It's so inspiring."

I ignored him with clenched teeth.

But of course he didn't let go. He raised his voice and repeated, "Baby, I said, show me again how to swing that hip. I'm here to learn, and you're here to teach."

The group stared at him.

A woman called Minnie started to giggle.

I fixed the Turtle with a stare as hard as I could. "My name is Karen."

"Oh, my, baby, I'm so sorry. I forgot. I thought you'd given me leave to call you some other names."

What could I say? Management has made it clear to me that I have to keep the customers happy no matter what. Every time I complain about the Turtle or other types, they suggest I "try a little harmless flirting." After all, the other instructors don't complain, so it must be me, right? Why, oh, why, do so many men think the skiing instructor is part of the package deal?

I closed my eyes and tried to remember why I love my job. The purple mountains. The air like chilled white wine. The joy of flying across the snow. Meeting many wonderful people, teaching them how to ski better. And the nasty ones don't stay long, so it's easy to bear. Usually.

I knew I had to put a stop to it right away; he would only make it worse if I lay down now. "I can't remember giving you permission to call me anything but Karen," I said, and I swished around to show them the arc once again.

Without giving them time for comment, I made them go through the motions. It's a mixed group, aged from thirteen to fifty, I would say. I'll separate them into beginners and advanced tomorrow. Unfortunately, I promised Steve to take the advanced group this time, and the Turtle is advanced—there's no denying that.

When I asked the Turtle to take his turn, he managed to brush against me, and then he yelled, "Oh, my, I'm so sorry, Kare-een, I lost my footing."

My face burned so much, it's a wonder I didn't melt a hole into the snow, but I clenched my teeth and didn't comment.

Next came the youngest of the group. He made a very creditable arc, and when he went past me on his way back, I said, "Well done."

The youngster cast me a glance and said in a low voice, "Don't mind that jerk."

From underneath his red cap two gray eyes fixed me earnestly. He has lashes every female would envy, thick and long and straight, and an adorable spattering of freckles across his nose.

I swallowed and promised myself to dispatch the Turtle somehow, to avoid spoiling that kid's Easter holiday.

So if you read about the murder of a turtle in the Teton Mountain Range, make sure you get me a good attorney, because it'll be hard to wriggle out of this one.

Love,
Karen

Dear Karen,

What a shame that the Turtle has turned into a regular. Maybe you should shove some leaflets with special offers from the competition under his door.

Am in a hurry. The contractor will be here in ten minutes to check the sagging kitchen floors, and I'm not even dressed!

Did you get No More Lies*? I posted it four days ago. Have fun reading, and tell me what you think!*

I've plowed my way through three-quarters of the books that came out in January but wished we could discuss them. This year I find it particularly hard to limit my choices. If only we had a larger store!

May seems so far away. Miss you.

Don't let the Turtle and his like disturb you too much.

Leslie

Dear Leslie,

I know you still have plenty of reading material and can live without a mile-long e-mail, but I have to write this letter; otherwise I'll burst.

It started with my sleeping late this morning. (Don't tell me you expected nothing better; I have improved in the past few years.) Besides, it's your fault, because you recommended *No More Lies,* and I couldn't stop reading until the wee hours, though I read at a pace that should have burned the pages. Thank you for sending it! I do agree, we have to get the author for a signing if we can. What do you think about a date sometime around the Fourth of July, when the crowds will be flocking to the Hamptons? I think it's perfect for our tourists.

Anyway, to get back to this morning: When the sunhine finally penetrated my mind, I realized that I'd better hurry if I didn't want to have twenty people waiting and complaining to management. So I skipped breakfast and ran to the lift.

In my hurry, I'd forgotten the Turtle. (Did I tell you his real name is Howard?) It felt like a punch in the stomach when I discovered his pasty face in front of me. "Here's our be-yootiful teacher," he crooned, "to show us things."

The way he pronounced *things* made my skin crawl. You know what I hate about him? He's making me feel helpless. There's nothing in his words I can complain about; it's just the way he says them. I can already hear myself telling management that he calls me "beautiful." They'll roll over laughing and tell me I should learn to accept a compliment gracefully. Ahhhh.

I ignored him as usual and kept the students busy with several exercises that showed me soon enough how to divide the group. The woman named Minnie deserves her name. She's a fluffy-head if you ever saw one, and she giggles more than should be legally allowed. But I have to be fair—she's too good to put with the beginners, so I'll have loads of giggles floating around me in the next two weeks. Maybe I can team her up with Howard, so they might offset each other.

The youngster—his name is Gerry, by the way—is a little too good for the beginners group but not quite strong enough for the advanced, so I hesitated. But since his father absolutely belongs in the advanced group, I put him there too.

I can already hear you say I made a bad choice, since kids that age prefer to be far away from their parents. Normally, I'd agree with you, but in this case, I got the impression that Gerry likes to be with his father. He looks at him in a way I can't describe but certainly not like the lot in my previous group, who ignored their parents as much as they could.

So I put him into the same group as his dad, and he beamed a smile at me that made it feel worthwhile to meet a Turtle every now and then. His grin was a triumph made flesh, and guess what—he's got dimples.

I know, I know. You'll roll your eyes and say I shouldn't fall for every guy with dimples, but I tell you, there aren't many around who can boast this feature. Not nearly enough, in fact. And I'm not falling for Gerry; I'm about twenty years older than he is.

You're asking me about his father? Well, until then I had barely noticed him, having my hands full with Howard and Gerry and Minnie. . . .

But that changed immediately.

After separating the lambs from the goats, I handed over the beginners to Steve and herded my flock to the Shoshone lift, so we could take our first tour through Trick Town Terrain Park.

On our way, Gerry observed everything around him with huge eyes, soaking it all up. The powdery snow, glistening sun, the sharp air, the sky so blue, it looked unreal.

I knew how he felt, but I thought it strange that a boy his age would even notice, when usually all they focus on at that stage are their snowboards and their gang—scenery be damned. But compared to what followed, that wasn't odd at all.

Because next, I happened to glance at the father. He didn't seem to appreciate the scenery at all. He was watching his son, with a face so torn, so . . . No, *torn* is the wrong word. It was full of love, and of longing, and yet I thought I saw regret and something else that constricted my throat.

All at once, he tore his gaze away, and his eyes met mine. I felt like someone staring through a lit window into a private living room. My face took on a tomato-red hue (I could feel it!), and I hastily averted my gaze, scolding myself for having fanciful thoughts. Because the second our eyes met, his face went blank, and I wasn't sure if I had imagined it all.

His name is John, by the way. A name that fits. He looks reliable. And serious. You know what I mean. A clean face, a straight way of meeting your eyes, a determined jaw. I wonder how he came to have a son with a rascally grin like that.

We spent the morning with the usual exercises, and I was surprised that Howard the Turtle didn't repeat his attacks. Later, though, I understood. He had been too busy planning the next one.

Just as we were about to leave—by this time, I was so hungry, I would have eaten anything but a turtle—he pretended to faint. Get that. He dropped against me, rolling his eyes heavenward, and gasped in a stage whisper that almost caused an avalanche, "I'm feeling faint, Karen."

I had to hold on to myself not to drop him into the snow. He even smells like a turtle. No, I can't say I ever got close enough to one to tell for certain, but if I ever do (which I'll try to avoid), I'm sure it'll smell like that: dust with a few rotten leaves thrown in.

"Pull yourself together . . . Howard," I said, remembering just in time not to call him *Turtle*. "We'll be down in a minute."

He snuggled his face into my chest in a way that made me gag. Before I could decide to drop his dead weight in spite of all the problems that act could cause with management, someone lifted him from me and pulled him to his feet.

It was John.

I told you he was reliable. I almost cheered.

Without ceremony, John bent the Turtle forward at the midriff, holding him much like a rag doll, and commanded: "Breathe deeply. In . . . out . . . in . . . out."

Howard struggled, his face red, but John held on and said in a voice devoid of emotion, "Relax. You shouldn't stand up too soon."

I bit my lip to suppress a grin. Then I met John's eyes.

They held a smile and an understanding that all at once made me feel I could deal with several turtles as long as he was there too. It was strange. I wondered if maybe he *wasn't* boring after all.

What do you think?

Karen

Dear Karen,

Hurray for John! Now you've got something to throw onto the scales when the Turtle becomes too much to bear. You'd better be careful, though. A man like that is likely to be married. I bet his wife is afraid of snow or heights, and that's why she didn't join them. Otherwise, go ahead and have fun! You deserve it!

Did I tell you the contractor finally came to see my house? He had slicked-back hair, so oily, I had to avert my eyes. You won't believe what he said. He prodded around, lifted a bit of the floor, held a beeping, high-tech something to my poor boards, straightened, and said, "I'm afraid you'll have to rip out the whole floor." CAN YOU BELIEVE IT? I'm off to find another contractor, one who is ready to condemn that judgment as completely off-the-mark.

Continue to write! I want to know everything! I love the way you make me feel as if I'm right next to you.

Leslie

Dear Leslie,

The whole floor? I can't believe it! Did he give you a reason? I do hope he was just trying to make money. Inform me as soon as you know more.

Here's my news, to distract you from your woes:

This morning, I managed to get up in time for breakfast. And guess who was sitting at my table when I came down? No, it wasn't the Turtle—trust Candy to have remembered that I don't like him.

She had picked Gerry and John. I was delighted.

On the other hand, it was kind of mean to them, because they won't have much fun with me in the mornings. I think the main reason my marriage with Rob failed is because the very idea of talking over coffee and toast across a breakfast table day after day makes me cringe.

Gerry, foolhardy enough, tried to strike up a conversation by asking me if I liked to be a skiing instructor but soon realized that philosophy at the breakfast table is not my forte. John, on the other hand, seems to be a man who recognizes danger with unerring instinct. He concentrated on refilling my cup in admirable silence.

While I tried to keep my eyes open and waited for the caffeine to kick in, I happened to glance at him. A smile played around his lips, as if he could do an impression of Fred Astaire at six on any given morning, followed by an invigorating algebra exercise. Yuk.

Hope I'll have a chance to prove to him that I can still do both at one A.M. on any given night, when he'll be dead on his feet, longing for his soft bed and a snore in a soothing rhythm.

I spent the evening in the kitchen, poring over maps with Candy. We're so excited about our cross-country trip in April. The only worry I have is that she might be tempted to drag me into every shopping center we pass. I mean, two to five is all right, but not ALL of them. When I told her so, Terry, her husband, who was reading the newspaper, snorted in an I-don't-think-you-can-prevent-her way and said he was glad his fishing trip did not require any shopping or sightseeing.

Candy patted his knee.

I said, "I know. I can't imagine how I ever came to be so demented as to prefer a car trip across a few states when instead I could have chosen to watch the surface of a lake that barely moves for hours."

Terry grinned and told me to cut it out before plunging into his newspaper again.

They're such a restful couple and so committed to each other. I admit that the way they treat each other does not make you think that they have sessions of wild passion on the kitchen floor, but that might be a bit cold anyway.

They work so hard, and I admire them for it. Can you imagine cleaning seven bathrooms every single morning? If it was my job, I'd ask for the shortest way out.

But Candy does it with eternal good cheer, singing and humming all the time. And it's due to her that people come back to the guesthouse every year, much like migratory birds, only the other way around.

What else is there to report?

Oh, yes, a major improvement:

During the last weeks, Terry added a much-needed mud-room to the side entrance for storing all our skis and boots. He also placed benches along the walls, so we won't fall like axed trees when wrestling with those icy boots. Hurray! Then he fixed hooks on the walls, so you don't even have to take your polar-bear outfit upstairs anymore. The place looks a bit like a gym now.

But Candy is a farseeing woman. She thought we might end up fighting over those hooks (after all, nobody arrives with only one jacket at a skiing holiday), so she thought up fancy names for each guest room, and these names now grace both the doors of every room *and* the hooks.

I think she has gone a bit over-the-top with those names. John and Gerry are staying at the "Sunset Suite" (guess why), and the Turtle has the same room as last year, which is named the "Terrarium."

No, just kidding.

That would have been my contribution to the baptism, but Candy was adamant and did not allow it. So it's the "Blue Saloon," and I guess that works just as well, as turtles need that special blue light to be happy . . . or do I have that mixed up with those southern flowers?

Anyway, I'm glad she doesn't tell her guests about the names in advance, as they might get the wrong impression. I mean, it's a lovely house, perfect for Teton Valley, with its huge pine logs that smell of resin when the sun is heating it up.

But it's not a castle, as the names might lead you to infer.

There's just one name that fits: My attic is simply called the "Nest," as Terry said it's too small to qualify for any other name.

But that's not all.

Oh, no. If Candy changes something, she throws herself into it with all her heart. So—to top it all off—she drove to Alta and purchased countless felt slippers, because she thought it would make life easier: for us, not freezing our little toes off when leaving our boots in the mudroom, and for her, not having to clean so much.

It's a voluntary thing, of course, but the guests squeal with glee when they discover the slippers. And so we're all slithering around as if we're visiting an old German castle. The slippers are all way too large because Candy only bought two sizes: a few for kids (a tiny five-year-old should fit) and the largest ones available at the store.

She said that with only two sizes, there would be no discussions or fights about them.

Too right. Only I suspect the decrease of injuries due to avoiding the "felled-tree phenomenon" is going to be offset by the increase of injuries that arise due to guests falling out of their slippers. (Cool sentence, eh? I sound like a textbook for young insurance brokers.)

But we'll see.

For now, it's new and fun, and you can't imagine how chummy you feel with a person you've never seen before in your life when he or she slithers next to you toward the breakfast table.

Heartfelt greetings from Teton Valley.

Karen

Dear Karen,

Those felt slippers sound wonderful! How I envy you! It must be heaven to glide across strong floors in top condition while I tiptoe around my kitchen, hoping I won't break through the boards.

I have invited two other specialists to check the floor. They will both come at the beginning of next week. Keep your fingers crossed for me.

Say hi to Candy and Terry from me. I know what you

mean, though for me, nothing but the sex-on-the-kitchen-floor kind of passion would do. (Ouch! I guess I should say bathroom *floor, since the* kitchen *floor might just cave in!)*

Talking about love, though: Lighten up, girl. Enjoy those two good-looking males at your breakfast table, try to flirt a bit, and take it easy. Not too much "philosophy," okay? And keep me posted on any developments.

Leslie

Dear Leslie,

You'll never believe what happened today. I took my group to Fred's Mountain, in the chairlift called Dreamcatcher. It was a bit early—we could have stayed on the lower slopes for another day—but I longed to see the view again.

Sometimes a yearning comes over me that pulls me to the top of Fred's mountain, as if I was bound to it by an elastic band. I'm hauled in like a stubborn mule. Not that I'm all that stubborn—I'm just sometimes too busy to obey right away.

Oh, I was so happy on the summit today! The air was clear, so I could see the valley way below, spot every little house, admire the roads snaking like black ribbons. I love the tiny cars running around like colorful blobs, looking so busy.

But the best thing was that I was far away and high above it all, feeling that all the hustle and bustle down there is the play version and that the real life is here, in the mountains, with the air biting your cheeks and the snow crunching beneath your skis. . . .

I admit I got distracted a little and stood dreaming for a while instead of correcting the Turtle's loops. When I came to myself with a start, I found John's eyes watching me. As if he could see right into my soul. I turned away. We're quits now. He shouldn't do that again.

Really.

I delayed returning to the valley until the sun went down. I know we stayed too long, but I couldn't resist. My group didn't complain, though some will have stiff muscles tomorrow.

Did you know that you can always tell what kind of a person someone is by observing them when they watch a sunset?

I think I should write a book about it and become famous.

Here's an excerpt: If they continue to practice, their teeth clenched, they're ambitious. Yes, yes, sorry, I know you figured that out without the explanation. A man called Rowland is like that. He would continue to practice even if a monkey crawled out from beneath a Douglas fir and asked the way to the local pharmacy.

Then there are people who will stop and take a glance for a fraction of a second and giggle before reorganizing their sunglasses and shaking their fragrant hair. Yes, you got that right: Minnie, of course.

There are others (I won't name names) who take a squint full of contempt out of their reptilian eyes at the lilac clouds and manage to hurl, "Kareeen, I think my boot laces got loose, and my fingers are frozen, and I can't fix them. Can you help me?"

Do you know who saved me this time? Gerry did. Without a word, he dropped to his knees and pulled at those laces until he got red in the face, and the Turtle recoiled. I expected that foot to fall off within one hour.

To return to the sunset-watching habit: Most people, I am relieved to say, stand still, in awe, swept away by the bold strokes of color, right across the silent giants—Mount Owen, Grand Teton. Aren't they lovely names? I really don't know why they had to give my favorite mountain the name Fred. It sounds so down-to-earth. They tried to offset the effect by tagging on the Dreamcatcher lift, but, honestly, would you feel like catching a dream when going to see "Fred"? I'm getting distracted again.

I wanted to tell you about the last sunset watcher: One man stood still and scowled. Isn't that strange? I wondered why he should scowl at the sunset. But I made sure I didn't meet his eyes, as I didn't want another soul-searching look to pass between us.

With all my watching and musing, we arrived last at the lift. I avoided sharing a cabin with Howard by pushing him bodily in with Rowland and Minnie and some others. A lovely mix. I then stopped to chat with Bruce, who finished up for the night before taking his snowmobile down to the valley. I got into the last car that left, together with Gerry and John (sometimes the gods are kind to helpless ski instructors).

We were moving for less than two minutes when, all at once, we stopped. Our little metal box hung suspended between heaven and earth and trembled a little, emitting one last protesting creak.

How comfy.

Gerry threw a scared look upward.

"It's all right," I said. "The cars barely ever fall down. Just two out of five every season."

His eyes widened. But then he got it (thank God) and chuckled.

Leslie, I have to go. My eyes are drooping, and I can't type anymore. I'll tell you more about it tomorrow. . . . At least you'll know I survived (unfortunately, so did the Turtle), but in another sense, it was quite unsettling.

Karen

Chapter Two

Karen!

How mean of you to leave me hanging in limbo! Do get back to that keyboard NOW, and tell me what happened! What was so unsettling?

Leslie

Dear Leslie,

Sorry! I didn't intend to be "mean" yesterday. I simply couldn't go on; my body overcame my feeble senses. . . . I'm not made out of the stuff it takes to become a Mahatma Gandhi.

Where was I? Oh, yes, we had just realized we were stuck in our chairlift car with darkness falling around us. I stretched out my legs with all the grace my clumpy boots allowed and settled back, surveying the two men in front of me. John seemed unruffled (I wonder what it takes to ruffle him), but Gerry's gaze darted here and there. He first probed the distance to the ground, then checked the cable above with a face that showed a mixture of mistrust and excitement. And suddenly I remembered I still

15

had to reply to his question at the breakfast table. "You asked me if I liked being a skiing teacher," I said.

He seemed embarrassed, remembering my unresponsive reply earlier, so I apologized and told them I wasn't a morning person (as if they hadn't noticed by now).

Again that superior Fred Astaire/algebra-exercise smile appeared at John's mouth. Humph.

I looked at Gerry. "I love my job."

Now I had his full attention. His gaze riveted on me as if it didn't matter that we were sitting in a softly swinging chairlift with no means to get to the ground. He wanted to know what my parents had said when I told them I wanted to become a skiing teacher.

At this point I realized something was afoot here, but I didn't quite grasp it. I shrugged. "Well, my dad sort of faded into the woodwork when I was four, so it was only me and my mother. And she . . ." I glanced from John's face, a study in marble, to Gerry's avid one and wondered how on earth I could avoid getting between them. Finally I went for the truth. "She said I shouldn't do it."

Gerry's eyes lit up. "But you did?"

"Yeah, I did." I could see that John would not need much encouragement to wring my neck if I continued in that vein, but I wasn't going to lie for him, though he continued to spear me with that stare. Boy, I tell you, I felt like a scared rabbit.

Gerry leaned back with a triumphant glance at his father. Suddenly he sat up again. "And what do you do in the summer?"

I was glad I could even out the situation with my reply. "In the summer, I do what my mother advised me to do."

His face fell, but John's stony edges got softer—marginally so, like a rock in water after a thousand years.

Gerry pulled himself together and asked, "What's your summer job, then?"

Clearly, he expected me to say that I did some office job, like typing information leaflets about how to insert dentures into water glasses for proper cleaning or something equally exciting. When I told him I owned part of a tiny bookstore, Gerry looked blank, and all at once I realized that, for him, a job at a bookstore might be on a par with typing stupid leaflets all day long, when for us, it's a lot more exciting than . . . . say, scuba diving.

John then joined the conversation for the first time and asked me where our shop was. When I said the Hamptons, he arched his eyebrows. "How nice. The sea in summer and the mountains in winter."

"You don't need to make it sound as if it wasn't a proper job," Gerry fired back.

I was surprised. John hadn't said it like that at all; he had sounded like most people do—a bit envious.

So I had been right: Something was wrong here. But before I could open my mouth, John said to me, "I'm sorry. I didn't mean to sound deprecatory."

At that moment, I saw him for the first time. Can you believe it? A man who's able to say "I'm sorry" without a problem. A man who doesn't box his son's ears when he's misbehaving but who wonders instead if said son might be right.

I was speechless. And discovered that they have the same gray eyes. Same lashes too. Wasted on a man like him, really. "You didn't sound deprecatory," I assured him.

Gerry got beet red.

It sure isn't easy, balancing between those two males, not understanding the undercurrents, each of them so complex and sensitive. To distract Gerry from his defeat, I asked him what he wanted to do after graduation. Major mistake. The second the words passed my lips, I wished I had kept my big mouth shut. As if it hadn't been clear since the beginning of the conversation that this topic was about as combustible as gasoline.

With a defiant glance at his father, Gerry said, "I want to become a musician."

Now I could see why this topic was so hot. Few parents start to cheer when their kids tell them they want a career in music.

I tried to think about a change of topic to get myself out of the mud without giving Gerry the impression that I couldn't care less, but it was too late already.

"I play the sax," Gerry said, much as he would announce that he's the guy who carries around the Olympic fire.

"That's great." I prayed the stupid car would start to move again and added for good measure, "I'm sure it won't be long now before the car will start to move again."

Gerry ignored my remark for the inane chatter it was. "I believe," he said, the freckles across his nose wrinkling, "you have to follow your dreams. Always."

Ooh-ah. At that point I wondered if maybe I should jump out, straight into the wooded slope below, figuring it might be less dangerous.

John rose to the bait, as he was supposed to do. "Of course it's important to follow your dreams," he said. "But you should never close off other avenues before you know for sure which one you want to take."

Gerry balled his fists. "But I keep telling you! I know it!" He fixed me with his look, his gaze pleading. "You did it too. You followed your dream, though your mother didn't want you to."

I had no clue how to wriggle out of this, so I dragged in my other career and told him I was also a trained librarian because my mother had recommended it. Okay, so it hadn't been a hardship, as my nose had always been in a book, but I didn't tell him that.

Gerry's face fell. He had counted on me as a fellow fighter. And now I had dropped the spear. How disappointing. He pushed his chin forward, making me want to take him into my arms to comfort him. "But why was your mother against your being a skiing instructor? Seems stupid to me."

"Because as a skiing instructor," I replied, "you have to remain polite to any old turtle, you have to work long hours on weekends and holidays, you have few chances to get a promotion, you're not paid very well, and when you're older than forty, you will feel it in your bones and will know that you have to look elsewhere double-quick if you don't want to eat dry bread crusts in the future."

I'm afraid my voice got a little bitter toward the end. When I glanced up, I found John watching me with that soul-seeing look again, and I added with all the speed I could muster, "There are benefits, though. You're not likely to die of a heart attack, with all the exercise you get."

At that instant, the car shuddered and moved an inch forward. We all raised our heads and scanned the ceiling, as if there was anything to see. Without making a sound, the night had crept onto us, pressing black against the windows.

Another shudder, another inch.

And then we were running again! Sometimes the gods do send angels who have a knack with electricity.

When we got off the ski lift, Howard immediately collared me and told me he would complain to the management of the Teton Valley Ski Tours about my inefficiency and the way I had delayed the group until the lift's electricity got cut off for the night. He said he could already feel a sore throat coming on, clutching his neck with more dramatic talent than Sarah Bernhardt.

I nodded and pretended to listen with a concerned face, wondering at the same time if management could believe the power cut to be my responsibility. I know, I know, it sounds far-fetched, but they've been so unreasonable in the last few months that I wouldn't put it past them. I only hope Howard's invented sore throat will make it difficult for him to speak much for the next few days. I'll remind him of it.

The other members of the group were kind of blue around

the nose. Minnie jumped from one foot to the other, hugged herself, and said with a chilled giggle that she was frozen to the core.

Funny. I hadn't felt a thing.

I really have to go to bed now because I need my wits about me tomorrow at breakfast between those two difficult males. I have a feeling Gerry won't let go of his favorite topic without another attempt to get support from someone with a fragile career in skiing, next to which music sounds thoroughly presentable.

What do the floor specialists say?

Karen

Dear Karen,

I got the felt slippers today, and, oh, I love to glide around in them. It's a bit like skating. Thank you so much! They saved me from utter despair because those two specialists were here today. One was very tasty, all muscles and dark hair, and we flirted a bit until he said the floor had to come out. I decided then that his brain must be in a much worse condition than his upper torso.

Unfortunately, the next specialist said the same. It seems the first owners of the house didn't impregnate the wood in the right way. Now it's rotten. Would you mind very much if I contacted Rob and asked him for a cost estimate? He's the best carpenter I know, but I won't if it makes you feel bad.

Keep out of that father-son fight, Karen. Just sail along, enjoy the company, but don't get too involved. Remember the wife. Remember to enjoy life, but make sure you keep your heart intact. Remember, you said independence is the most important thing in your life. Right?

Leslie

Dear Leslie,

I'm glad you liked the felt slippers and that they came just when you needed them! Of course I don't mind if you ask Rob. I don't have to be around when he's doing the repairs, so there's no danger of any ex-husband/wife fight anyway! Did you ask the specialists if the kitchen is the only floor that needs to be exchanged? If it's a matter of missing impregnation, it's not very likely that the previous owners impregnated part of the house and stopped when they came to the kitchen, is it?

Sorry for that nasty thought. I'm thinking of you . . . if I can help in any way, do tell me.

Today was calm—well, if you don't count the fact that Minnie got stuck in her glove. I think I'll tell you about it, so you'll have something to make you smile.

We had just returned to the guesthouse and were busy getting out of our heavy gear in the mudroom, when Minnie turned red in the face, fighting with a glove.

"What's the matter?" I asked.

"This stupid glove!" she said with a nervous giggle. "I can't take it off."

I went to her and tried to pull it off, but she was right: It was stuck. And stuck it remained, no matter what we did. I tried shaking and lifting and squeezing, but we made no progress at all.

In the meantime, the others had built a fascinated circle around us. "You'll have to cut off the glove," Rowland said.

As it was an expensive leather glove with real lamb's wool lining, I didn't blame Minnie for throwing a glance at Rowland that, by rights, should have annihilated him.

"Gosh," Gerry said with badly hidden glee, "will she have to sleep in it?"

His father grabbed him by the scruff of his neck and mildly shook him, but I'm afraid we all had to suppress a grin.

Minnie, however, didn't think it was funny. She wasn't even giggling anymore.

"Here, let me do it," the Turtle said, and he pushed me out of the way.

But ten minutes later, when everybody had finished trying, the glove was still on her hand, and Minnie looked as if she was about to burst into tears. "Whatever can it be?"

Something dawned on me. "Do you happen to be wearing a big engagement ring?"

"Well, yes . . ."

"There you go. Your precious stone worked itself into the lining, and that's why you can't get the glove off. I've seen it happen before, but never like this."

Suddenly I had an idea. I ran to the kitchen and returned with one of the long skewers Candy uses for shish kebab.

Minnie recoiled, and I think Gerry would have cheered, mistaking my action for a wintry kind of bullfight, if John hadn't stopped him with a sharp look.

I inserted the skewer with care and tried to lift the fabric all around her ring. It took ages, as I only moved the spit in tiny fractions around the material because I was so afraid of hurting her. At long last we managed to ease the glove off.

Minnie fell around my neck in gratitude.

I said, "Better take off your ring and store it in a safe at the bank during your stay. Engagement rings weren't made for ski gloves. Or any other practical thing, come to think of it."

At that instant Howard said to Minnie, "But you're bleeding!"

I froze. And then I saw it. A slight bit of blood on Minnie's finger.

Howard's eyes threatened to fall out of his head.

Oh, God. Do you think management will say it diminishes my popularity if I spear an occasional student from time to time?

Karen

Dear Karen,

Loved the Minnie story! I hope the wound has healed in the meantime.

No, the other floors are fine. Apparently the ex-owners ran out of impregnating stuff when it came to the kitchen. I'm grateful for that. I would hate to get a loan for completely new flooring. There are so many wonderful things I would rather do with the money.

Have to run; the store has to be opened in three minutes! Keep writing!

Leslie

Dear Leslie,

Today I took my group to a cabin high on Peaked Mountain for lunch. I'm addicted to the sandwiches we get there. They're not just sandwiches, they're complete lunches in horizontal form: thick slabs of whole-wheat bread covered with mountain cheese and air-dried ham and crisp lettuce and those tomatoes that smell like a field in the sun.

We dropped into the deck chairs on the porch behind the hut with happy sighs and stretched out our legs. Is there anything better than the feeling of being truly hungry after a few hours of skiing? I love the contented weakness that settles into my legs after a morning on my skis, and the happiness in my stomach with the first bite that wanders down, and the sun glaring against my sunglasses, warming my skin until it tingles.

"If you were a cat, I would expect you to purr," a voice suddenly said next to me.

It was John. Of course. I thought his soul-seeing glances would be warded off by my sunglasses, but not so.

You say it's easy to read the mood of any person sitting in the sun as described?

You're wrong. Howard, for example, was busy writing in a notebook with an expression as intense as if he was trying to do a sum of the national debt. Maybe he was listing the insults he gets per day.

Rowland was stretched out to his full length, with his face turned to the sun, but his frown was so deep, he'll end up with a white crease between his eyes. I'm sure he's going through our exercises of this morning, flogging himself for every mistake he made.

So you see, it's not so obvious.

Besides, I was just about to glide off into dreamland, and my mouth had gone slack, no smile anymore. I'm sure it wasn't hanging open, though.

Certainly not.

I hope not.

Oh, God. I *had* heard my mouth closing with a snap. If it did that, it must have been open before, mustn't it? I think I'll refuse to think about it.

When I had finally gathered the weak strands of my wits about me, I replied, "Well, if you don't start to purr here, where would you?"

He smiled. "I wanted to ask you if you could recommend me another place to purr."

I must have looked a bit alarmed, because he hastily added, "I wanted to take Gerry to a restaurant tonight instead of staying at the guesthouse, and I wondered if you could tell me the best place in the Valley."

I was about to open my mouth and say the Blue Note but managed just in time to pull myself up short. Do you recall their jazz sessions? Within the last few years they've become known across the borders of Wyoming, and with a son playing sax and him against it, the Blue Note might not be a tactful place to recommend, even though the food is the best around ever since they got their new cook.

"Why don't you try Chez Martine?" I said instead, then instantly wondered if it was too expensive. But then I remembered his skiing outfit. It wasn't the Wal-Mart style, and even if he'd bought his and Gerry's stuff secondhand, he would not be reduced to penury by one evening out. Besides, he had asked me if one could purr there, and if you didn't purr after a meal at Martine, you never would.

All this talking about purring and eating made me wonder if I didn't want a change of scenery too, so that night I decided to treat myself to dinner at the Blue Note. Just a small one. After all, I had already saved all I would need for my cross-country trip with Candy (and a bit more, for additional shopping sprees), so I figured I could spoil myself a bit.

I celebrated the occasion by putting on my black sweater with the interesting neckline and brushing some gel into my curls so they would remember that being flattened by a woolen hat wasn't the style to wear this year.

Satisfied with myself, I careened like a stork out the door, because it's weird to walk without those heavy ski boots, and I always need a few minutes before remembering that I don't have to lift my feet so high if I don't have their weight on my limbs.

I wonder if I should stop now because your eyes will hurt already or if I should continue . . . but I can't hold on to myself, so brace yourself for another marathon letter. I don't know what's come over me, but if I don't tell you all about it, I'm going to start talking to my shampoo, and I doubt the shampoo will appreciate it. I'll try to give you a blow-by-blow account, so you'll be able to tell me what you think about it.

So, who do you think I met at the reception desk of the Blue Note?

Gerry and his father. I must have looked as if a celestial apparition loomed in front of me, because John immediately said, "Candy told us about the Blue Note, and I thought Gerry might like it even more than Chez Martine."

Garry's eyes shone. "Did you know that Lee Walters will be playing tonight?"

Lee Walters.

Have you ever heard of Lee Walters? I couldn't bring myself to deny any knowledge of him. Trying to think of a suitable reply, I noticed from the corner of my eye that John was amusing himself at my predicament, when Gerry suddenly bounced back to earth and said, "You'll join us at our table, won't you? Dad made a reservation in the front row yesterday."

Yesterday? He only asked me about a restaurant today. I shot a glance at John. Now it was his turn to scrutinize the floorboards as if they could offer lifesaving advice.

Odd.

Just as I opened my mouth, the receptionist came back and asked if John wanted a table for two or three. I took a deep breath.

Gerry said, "You'll join us, won't you?"

I wondered if I should claim a sudden weakness in the stomach.

Then I met John's eyes.

"I would be delighted," he said in a voice sounding so serious, it made me feel strange—hot and cool at the same time. Maybe I'm getting a cold.

The receptionist decided that nobody could refuse such an invitation, turned on her heels, and led us to a table at the front. I followed, not sure if I was being stupid.

John pulled out a chair for me and waited until I was seated. You know, I appreciate old-fashioned politeness. I know it's not logical, as I insist on being treated like an equal on every other occasion, but who says I always have to act in a logical way?

As soon as the hostess had vanished, I tackled him. "Why did you ask me about a restaurant if you'd already made a reservation?"

John looked uncomfortable. He stared at his hands, folded on the table, then at the stage with the deserted drums. Gerry's gaze darted from one to the other of us as if we were playing Ping-Pong, aware of every nuance in our words. He doesn't miss much, that boy, more's the pity.

Finally John met my eyes. "You had just fallen asleep in your deck chair."

My cheeks flamed. So my mouth *had* been open. Isn't that awful, Leslie?

Having crossed the first hurdle, John hurried on. "And Howard was watching you and making notes in his little book."

All at once, I got it. "You mean he made a note about my falling asleep?"

John nodded. "So I figured I'd better wake you up."

I was speechless. Can you imagine that? What a toad the Turtle is proving to be!

"He's disgusting!" Even Gerry's freckles looked angry. "Why are you so nice to him?"

I shrugged. "He's a customer. And I have management to please."

John's gaze searched my face. "And if you explained the situation to them?"

I leaned back in my seat and crossed my arms in front of my chest so the guys wouldn't see my trembling hands. "No chance. They'll only say I should take it easy."

I should have left it at that. But my bitterness got the better of me, and before I could stop myself, I said, "They keep saying that if I only knew how to flirt, I could manage men like him better."

John's eyebrows soared. "You don't know how to flirt?"

Leslie, what would you answer if a good-looking guy asked you if you knew how to flirt?

I know what you would do. You would lower your lashes and glance at him sideways and say, "It's all a question of the circumstances."

But I can't.

I just can't.

I don't know why it's like that, but as soon as I lower my lashes and glance at someone from the side, I look like a squinting tuna, and if I try a sultry voice, people offer me eucalyptus drops. So I glared at him, said, "No," with a voice gruffer than a grizzly bear's and prayed that he wouldn't offer to teach me.

The waitress saved me. By the time we had discussed the specials of the day and placed our orders, I had recovered my equilibrium sufficiently to start discussing the next day's trip. But not for long.

All at once Gerry's face fell, and his gaze riveted onto something behind my back as if a tarantula was crawling into the room. I stopped short in the middle of my sentence and whipped around.

Howard.

Right behind my chair.

For an instant it was touch and go. My fingers curled around my wineglass, and I was already lifting it, thinking how nice my red wine would look on the Turtle's white sweater, when John's hand came down over mine. His cool gray eyes bored into me, and he said, softly, so only I could hear it, "Don't. He's not worth it."

The Turtle smiled. Well, to be correct, he made some movement of his mouth that was supposed to pass for a smile and said, "I told the hostess that we're all part of the same group and that you would surely find a little room for me." He made a sweeping movement with one long arm. "They're fully booked tonight."

I wanted to holler. How dare he come here! How dare he destroy our evening? Gerry's face turned pale; he looked as helpless as I felt. He had been looking forward to this evening so much. Why does ruthlessness always win?

Then I heard John's pleasant voice. "You're right, Howard, but tonight is an exception. You see, we're having a private party, and you would feel very awkward mixed up in it."

I held my breath.

Howard turned a bluish red, reminding me of a wrinkled plum. After a second he bared his teeth and said, "Let me be the judge of that."

"No," John said.

Leslie, you've never heard a similar "no." If we will be subjected to a final judgment one day, and if we should dare to ask if maybe, maybe, we can take one little sin to heaven with us, I imagine the "no" will sound softer.

And yet, John's voice was unruffled, his face relaxed. Then he leaned back, made a sign to the hostess, and when she came close, he said, "Could you try to find a table for Howard? We would very much appreciate it."

She's a professional; I have to grant her that. She met his eyes for a second, nodded, then schlepped the Turtle away.

I drew a cautious breath.

"Dad, that was brilliant," Gerry said. He fixed his father with shining eyes, then grinned. "But it wasn't polite. And you always say that no matter what happens, you have to remain polite."

John nodded with a rueful smile. "I know. But if sticking to the rules makes you a victim, then different rules might apply. I tried to let him down lightly, though."

I cleared my throat. "I'm sure he didn't appreciate that."

John looked at me. "No. He wouldn't," he said, "and there'll be more trouble yet, I'm sure. But let's forget him for now. He's not worth it."

So we tried to. But my whole focus had shifted. If I remember correctly, I described John as predictable, boring even. I've never been so wrong.

After our meals, the band started to play. I enjoyed watching

Gerry: He soaked it all up. His whole body moved with the rhythm, and any minute I expected him to jump up and join the musicians on the stage. John watched him too. And again I caught the tail end of the expression I had seen before, that mixture of sadness and love. I looked away, wishing I knew more about them.

When I dared another glance, I found he was watching me, but I couldn't tell from his face what he had been thinking. I smiled a little, and he smiled back, and all at once I wished we were friends.

When the band finished, Gerry jumped up and ran to the guy who played the sax (Lee Walters, was it?), involving him in a discussion that seemed to make both of them happy.

John watched him for a minute, then leaned back in his seat and stared at the glass in his hand.

I had to know. I took my courage in both hands and asked him why Gerry's career was such a big issue, him only being fourteen. He told me Gerry wants to switch schools, joining one that concentrates on developing musical talents, but he didn't know if it was a good move, because he has no way to judge if Gerry really is brilliant or just a bit better than the rest.

"So what do the music professionals say? His teachers?"

John shrugged. "Some say he's brilliant enough to make it; some are more cautious."

"And what does his mother say?"

He stared at me as if I had asked for the opinion of the guy at the local gas station. "His mother?"

"Yes."

"We're separated."

I was stunned. I told you he seemed like a guy well settled, didn't I? With his house and life and family exactly as he wanted it. I had gotten it wrong. Again. I pulled myself together. "But she has an opinion, doesn't she?"

"Oh, yes." A smile played around his lips; it didn't look amused. "She thinks he should study electronics."

I grabbed my chair to avoid falling off. "Electronics? Why?"

"Because then he can take over the family business."

"Is he interested in that at all?"

John shook his head.

I swallowed and decided to take the plunge and ask him. "Would you like it if he took over the business?"

He sighed. "Sure, I would like it. But if he doesn't want it, that's no problem either. You have to follow your dreams, right? That's what you did, and I have the impression it worked for you." A brief smile. "It was good for me too."

"Then why are you so set against that music school?"

"Because he's too young." He leaned forward. "What if he changes his mind in two years? What if he's not good enough? Does he want to play in mediocre bars for the rest of his life? It would break his heart."

I thought a while about my answer, remembering my fears when we started up our store, Leslie, remembering the year when we almost went bankrupt. Finally I said, "You can't protect your kids from heartbreak. Isn't it better to fight for your dream and break your heart over it than give up before you even try and break your heart being a mediocre electronics guy?"

His gaze dropped. He stared at the tabletop. It was quiet in the bar. Most customers had gone, but Gerry was still deep in his talk with the famous Lee.

Finally John lifted his head and met my eyes squarely. "If you could start all over again, would you choose the same career? Or *careers,* I should say."

You know what I said; I didn't even have to think about it. "Yes."

A smile lurked in his eyes. "In spite of the Howards?"

"I meet Johns and Gerrys too."

He got up. "Didn't you say you don't know how to flirt?"
I didn't reply. But do you know what scared me, Leslie?
I wasn't flirting.
Karen

Dear Karen,

Darling, of course I know Lee Walters. What on earth is he doing in the backwaters of Teton Valley? You really have to get out more!

I have to be short today, so here's my news in telegraph style. Got two cost estimates for the floor—Rob's was cheaper, and I know he does good work. He'll start tomorrow. Am busy moving the microwave to my bedroom, so I won't starve, and the rest of the kitchen into the storage unit I just rented. I HATE this.

One other thing: I know you don't like the carpet in the store, but could we keep it for another season? I would hate to exchange it now.

I won't write much in the next few days, but please keep me updated! I need to know how things proceed between you and those two guys. I hardly know what to say. Is this serious?

Leslie

Dear Leslie,

I keep seeing you in front of my inner eye, without anything warm to eat or drink. Buy some M&M's, will you? They'll tide you over.

You said you wanted continued news from the Teton Mountain Range, so here goes. Today, Terry said if Candy and I were going to be on the road all by ourselves for four weeks, then we should be able to change a tire on the car. He proposed a tutorial.

Candy and I exchanged a glance. I'm all for being independent, no doubt about it. But Terry had chosen a bad moment: The sun was about to set, and it had started to snow. When I pointed the weather out to him, he grinned and said you can't choose your moment when breaking down.

Right. I couldn't think of any other excuse; besides, there was a grain of truth somewhere in his statement.

So we bundled up in old clothes and trooped out. It only took us about twenty minutes of rummaging around in the garage before we found a flashlight strong enough to tell us where to find the spare tire. In the meantime, the night had turned pitch-black; only the dancing snowflakes sparkled whenever they frolicked into the beam of our flashlight.

It's not as if I'm a technical loser. Not at all. But did you know that the spare tire is hidden in the car trunk below a mechanism that was invented by the same guy who set up the security system of the State Treasury? It's easy once you know how to do it—in fact, a flick of the fingernail is enough—but it's not exactly self-explanatory.

And when you have finally managed to pry its secret out of it, you crack your back trying to lift that heavy tire.

But from then on it got better, and Candy and I were already telling each other what brilliant repair experts we were—a little prematurely, I admit, when it came to unfastening the four nuts holding each of the car's tires in place: We took a big wrench that's almost as long as my arm and pulled at the nuts with all our might. Three gave way after much protest, but the fourth resisted.

We tried it singly and together.

Nothing doing.

The nut laughed at us.

Suddenly a voice came from the shadows behind us. "Can I help you ladies?"

It was the Turtle.

"No, thank you." I gave the wrench another shove.

He came closer. "It's seems that nut is stuck, Kareeen."

"Yes," I said, wishing I knew how to get rid of him. I passed the wrench to Candy for another try.

The nut chuckled at her. I swear it.

Terry had kept himself in the background with the occasional teasing remark and sometimes helpful advice. He now came forward, his hands in his pockets, and said, "Don't worry, Howard. These two ladies will manage on their own." I couldn't hear the slightest undertone in his voice, and all at once I realized he had not engineered this session to get a rise out of us. He truly wanted us to be able to do it. Maybe he had visions of his Candy stranded on some highway, at the mercy of the next guy who drove by. I smiled at him.

"Ah, these are ladies who don't need men, I take it?" Howard said with a snicker.

Thank God Candy had gotten hold of the wrench by that time; otherwise, I would have dropped it onto his foot.

That very instant I heard Gerry's voice behind me. "Gosh, Karen, do you have a flat tire?"

"Kind of," I said. Darn. I didn't want the entire Teton Valley watching while Candy and I struggled through our first tire-changing lesson.

Gerry had already thrown himself toward Candy to help, when a hand shot out and held him back. "If I get it right, this is an exercise," John said. "So you'd better stay out of it."

I veered round. "How did you know?"

His dimples appeared. "That tire you're changing isn't flat."

I told you he sees a lot.

Howard blinked at the tire, then at us.

Candy straightened, her face hot and red.

If Howard hadn't been present, I would have asked Terry to help. After all, men are generally stronger than women; I'm not one to deny biological differences. But after that Turtle-snicker, I simply couldn't claim defeat.

"Hold the wrench in place, Candy," I said, "and mind your fingers. I'll try it with my foot."

I took careful aim and gave an almighty kick. Something crunched, and then the wrench flew away in a wide arc.

"It's loose!" I hopped around in the snow, triumphant as a crow with a worm. "We did it!"

John lifted the wrench. "Maybe you should pack a few spare ones of these, though."

We all whipped around and stared. The wrench had a bend in the middle. It was not quite a boomerang yet, but it was on the way.

Terry blinked. "Dear God," he muttered.

Across the wrench, my eyes met John's. An understanding smile played around his lips, and he said softly, "Isn't it amazing to what heights of achievement a single remark can push us?"

Darn. He must have overheard the Turtle.

Before I could think of a witty reply, John turned and shepherded Gerry and Howard away.

It took all of our strength to fasten the nuts again. When we had finished, Terry nodded, said we would manage, and unobtrusively tightened them another full turn or two. It was disheartening.

But it's good to know we can do it, even if it means we have to stop every two hundred yards or so to tighten the nuts.

Have you ever tried to change your tires, my dear?

Karen

Chapter Three

Dear Leslie,

I haven't heard from you and hope the work in your kitchen is proceeding well. I have to whine a bit today.

The Turtle is giving me the evil eye. Wherever I am, he is close to me. He stares at me with his half-closed, reptilian eyes and will not smile, no matter what I say. And I assure you, I am funny. At least, the rest of the group hardly stops laughing.

But not Howard, oh, no. He only hypnotizes me with that stare. I am soon going to scream and throw a ski pole at his head.

My only rescue is John. He blocks off the Turtle's attacks in a way I can't describe. It's done with so much ease, and yet there's no way you could take it as a soft rebuke. It's more like a wall, standing there as if it belonged there, and no mistake about it.

On the one hand, I love it and wish I could be like that. I tried to imitate it, but coming from me, it sounded all wrong, like a cuddly cat imitating a panther.

On the other hand, it scares me to death. I have come to

rely on his help, all within a few days! He has booked two weeks here, and the Turtle's stay is a week beyond that, so how am I going to manage the last week?

I hate to be dependent on someone. You know that. Ever since Rob, I've always managed on my own. And it's good that way.

I'm completely rattled by this turn of events.

So I tried to get some distance. Yesterday I didn't look at John when the Turtle got mean. Instead, I concentrated on being far away. I avoided riding with John and Gerry in the lift, and at lunch break I endured a full twenty-eight minutes of Minnie's giggling conversation.

But tonight, as I sat in front of my little woodstove, toasting my feet, I felt miserable. I mean, he's only staying two weeks, and he's the nicest guy I've met for a long time. So why do I turn and run in the other direction instead of enjoying his company?

To divert my mind, I trudged downstairs and got more wood for the little stove. Just as I entered the mudroom, where it smells of wet wool and apples, John came in from the other side. We both stopped. I was glad the only light in the room came from the hallway, behind John's back, because I think I blushed for no reason at all.

"Let me take that," he said.

Before I could reply, he relieved me of the heavy wood basket.

I stomped my feet to shake loose any snow I'd picked up and tried to figure out if I was pleased or annoyed. I couldn't tell.

By the time we arrived at the Nest, he was panting. He lowered his head (have I told you he's tall?) and schlepped my basket through the door. All at once my little room seemed full to bursting with me and him and the little stove.

He put down the basket and contemplated me, appearing thoughtful.

I stared at him, wondering what on earth he might be thinking. At some point I remembered my manners and said, "Thank you."

He brushed it aside. And suddenly he said, "Have I done anything to upset you?"

I believe my mouth dropped open. "Why . . . why do you think that?" I asked, to buy time.

"You're different," he said, his gaze never leaving my face.

I bent down and stuffed a chunk of wood into the little stove. What could I tell him? I couldn't very well admit that I was afraid of getting closer. Maybe he was only being friendly, and such a statement would scare him out of his skin.

But I couldn't lie to him either, Leslie. So I compromised on a half truth. "The Turtle rattles me."

"What?"

I had forgotten that only you knew Howard's nickname, and I told him.

He grinned. "An apt name."

I smiled back. And all at once everything relaxed between us, back to the way it was before.

He sensed it too; I could tell by the way his shoulders eased. He looked around. "It's a cozy place."

"With you inside, it's rather full."

He arched his eyebrows. "Do I take that the way it sounds?"

Oh, God, I think I blushed again. Trust me to put my foot in. "No, no, I'm sorry, I just wanted to say it's small." To change his skeptical expression, I added, "It's much larger than my other place, though."

"You mean on Long Island?"

I nodded. "I've got a tiny trailer over there."

That got him. He stared at me as if I had declared that my usual abode was a muddy hole in the ground, and he asked me why I chose to live like that.

"Because I love it."

I could see he didn't get it. Few people do. I mean, even you keep asking me if I don't want to find something bigger.

"Won't you sit down?" I motioned toward the only easy chair. When he hesitated, I took the fat cushion from the top of my bed, dropped it onto the floor, and sat on it, with my legs crossed under me.

I'm happy to report that John fits much better into my place when folded into a sitting position. When we had fit him in, I took a deep breath and said, "I'm a gypsy. A half-domesticated gypsy. Can't imagine living all year 'round in the same place." I went on to explain all about the expense of keeping two apartments if you only live in each one half the year and how I got the attic from Candy and paid for making it habitable so I only pay a low rent now. I also told him about my trailer, closed away in a shed in winter, and about my two months of vacation each year.

He raised his eyebrows at that, and I had to grin. I explained my two "shifts," teaching skiing from mid-November to the beginning of April and working at our bookstore from May to autumn. I couldn't stop myself from telling him every detail about my cross-country trip with Candy this April. Ha, I've just realized I haven't told YOU every detail yet—hurray, another victim! We'll start with the West Coast, then down to California, all the way to Mexico, then up again via the Rocky Mountains. Doesn't that sound fantastic? When I told John, I could feel a happy smile breaking out of every pore. It's a perfect life.

When I said that, he looked at me with the soul-seeing gaze that always makes me feel much too transparent. Everything I had said was true. Maybe I had flung it out too defiantly? Though I have no reason at all to be defiant, none at all. After all, that's how I want it to be.

He tilted his head to one side, a frown gathering on his face. "What about roots?"

"Roots?"

"Yeah. People."

I swallowed. He was getting way too close for comfort. I pointed at my laptop, sitting on my bed. "I keep in touch via e-mail. I have close friends in both places. Leslie, my partner at the bookstore. And Candy here. And it's not as if I'm gone for years and years. I always come back."

He watched me in his thoughtful way, and suddenly I knew what he wanted to know and that he wouldn't ask because it would be too intimate. So I gave him the answer and decided not to think too much about my reasons.

"I tried to settle once. Rob, my ex-husband, has a small vineyard on Long Island besides being a carpenter, and . . . and I really tried to make it work."

"But?"

"But I was miserable. I made him miserable. We were married for two years. Before it ended in a catastrophe, I stopped the whole thing."

"And now you've got all you want?"

He didn't ask that as if he doubted it. He asked as if he was deep in his own thoughts, as if he really wanted to know, not to challenge me but to understand. I'm not sure if you understand what I'm trying to say—it probably sounds muddled— but I can't express it any better. Anyway, I wasn't going to answer that one. Couldn't, even if I wanted to. So I decided to turn the tables and said, "Have you got all you want?"

His gray eyes locked with mine. And slowly, as if he had just discovered it, he said, "No. No, I don't."

I got up. "But I bet you have what you want most. Life is all about making choices. Often it's unconscious, but I have learned that, in general, everybody stays true to form." I grinned at him to lighten the mood. "At least, I do."

At that moment, a bumping sound came from the stairs, and when I called, "Come in," Gerry, in his felt slippers, fell across the threshold.

"Here you are!" he said to his father, like a mother scolding a child who had wandered off.

John unfolded himself from the chair. Immediately the room was full again. Gerry's eyes grew wide. "Gosh, this place is tiny." He moved a step closer, and now it was definitely overcrowded. He stared at me. "How can you stand it?"

"I like it."

"You like it? How can you like it? There's barely enough room to turn around."

John's hand shot forward and grabbed Gerry's shoulder, but it was too late.

I had to laugh. "I don't usually cram two additional men into it, and if I stick to that simple rule, I'm fine."

"But you can't . . ."

John interrupted his son before he could make it worse and, with an apologetic glance at me, propelled him out the door and left.

Will now go to bed and think about the choices you make in life, and about being happy.

Good night,

Karen

P.S. I really think the old carpet should go. I know it's awful timing for you, but if we leave it another season, our customers are bound to catch their feet in one of those nooses that tend to undo themselves. And when I said they should stay riveted in our store, I didn't mean it literally.

Dear Karen,

Did John understand that you love your life and that sitting in one place all year 'round won't do at all? I've never met anybody as fiercely independent as you are. It defines you. I've no clue where this will lead, but please take care of your heart. You tend to take things so seriously. Couldn't you just go back to that light flirtation and a hot kiss or two?

On a more positive note: I found some kind of super-glue that fixes the nooses forEVER, so we needn't worry about being sued by stumbling customers, and the carpet can STAY!

Leslie

Dear Leslie,

All right for the carpet. As long as the glue dries quickly. Imagine if the customers got stuck to our floor. . . .

I believe Terry is not one hundred percent easy about letting his Candy stray across the US with me. He asked us today which routes we plan to take, and when the table in the kitchen proved to be too small, we moved to the breakfast room, where we spread out all the maps.

I brought down my guidebooks, and while Candy showed Terry every inch we plan to cover, I got lost in my books and pleasurable dreams, only waking up occasionally to dig my elbow into Candy's side and say, "Here, you have to read this!"

I'm particularly looking forward to driving along the coast of the Pacific Ocean, the scenic drive between SF and LA everybody raves about. Will have to bribe Candy to drive at that moment or, better yet, will have to convince her to drive the same stretch up and down twice, so we can take turns. After all, it all looks different if you come from another direction, doesn't it?

Terry looked horrified when I suggested it, and Candy asked how many malls we would be able to cover on that particular stretch. I swallowed and wondered if maybe I am making a mistake.

Just as Candy brought us large mugs of hot chocolate and

M&M's (trust her to remember the essentials), Gerry prowled in. He has a built-in GPS that guides him unerringly toward sources of food. Officially, though, he was looking for a sweater he claimed to have lost during breakfast.

As Candy has fallen for him hook, line, and sinker (can't imagine why), he got his own cup of cocoa and joined our discussion. Seems he has been to Big Sur on a previous vacation and could tell us a bit about it.

As his directions were rather hazy, though, it was a good thing that John arrived shortly afterward in search of his son.

I had been on the lookout for him and should not have been surprised when he walked in, but my heart behaved as if my brain hadn't passed on that particular information.

He pulled up a chair next to me and managed to elucidate a few of Gerry's comments I had found rather puzzling.

The more John explained about the scenic drive, the more excited I got, and even Candy caught fire. We changed our route according to his suggestions twice, me taking notes and munching M&M's, and it wasn't long before I wanted to jump up, fling my suitcase into the trunk, and drive off that same minute.

We were deep in our discussion when the telephone rang, and Terry got up to answer it. Candy used the break to refill our mugs in the kitchen (Gerry trailing along, in hopes of scrounging a few more M&M's), so I was left with John.

Our eyes met. A smile deepened in those gray eyes of his, and all at once he reached out, cupped my chin lightly, and said, "Do you know you're beautiful with your red cheeks and shining eyes?"

I stared at him and said—well, you know what I said.

Nothing, of course. I'm nil at flirting, and I fear that will never change. (It's all right for you to say I should attempt a small flirtation. You're the world's best flirter; you've no idea how hard it is.) I only managed a small smile, I think. Great.

A second later Terry came back, and we turned once more to

our maps, but my notes from then on proved to be unreadable, as I discovered later.

But the worst is that I think I caught a movement out of the corner of my eye at the open door, and if I'm not mistaken, the Turtle might have peered in at the wrong moment.

Hallelujah.

Karen

Dear Karen,

I note that you never reply to any deeper questions in my e-mails. All right. I know what that means. It might be too late for me to say "Take it easy," so I guess I'll stop preaching, but I'm thinking of you. Picture me with a worried frown . . . and not because of the Turtle. If he should dare to make problems, refer him to me; I'll give him a piece of my mind.

My house is covered with sawdust, but I can see some progress. Everything smells of freshly cut wood.

Have to run.

Leslie

Dear Leslie,

I haven't told you yet where John and Gerry live, have I? Well, guess! Go back a few years . . . well, quite a few years, to be exact.

Think mud.

Think trees.

Think collapsing tent.

No, I can see you don't get it.

Okay, so think of that lanky guy with virtually no hair at all, it was cut so short. What was his name? Greg? Matt? The one you were so crazy about, everything else just slipped your mind, and you insist to this day it was the best holiday we ever had. Weren't you even pen pals for a year or two?

Yes.

Seattle.

I shuddered when they told me, and of course John noticed and asked if I was cold. I pretended I was.

Couldn't very well tell him that Seattle was, to me, the incarnation of hell, only toward the cold and wet end.

But with the exception of that bad moment (I've made sure not to talk about Seattle with them anymore), we're having a great time.

Gerry seems to be distracted by the skiing, so we didn't have any further discussions about the music school. Which is good, as there tends to be a tension-laden atmosphere whenever the subject is mentioned.

Isn't it funny how you can be with some people for years and never get closer, and how you can meet someone else and, within no time at all, you know you've found a friend? It's such a delicious feeling.

Karen

Dear Karen,

Seattle! Wow—what a fantastic place! Try to get yourself invited! And don't you dare make fun of my old pen pal. I loved him to bits, only his letters stopped at some point. Men.

Leslie

Dear Leslie,

When we returned from classes today, Candy came running out to us and asked if we had heard it already. My hands gripped the ski poles like some lifeline. And then she told us.

I immediately rushed inside and tried to call you, but I got no answer at the store, and even your cell was switched off. Oh, God.

How bad is it? They showed pictures on TV, about the

waves being as high as houses right up to Shinnecock Bay. They say a storm like that has never hit Long Island before.

I do hope you're safe.

Call me!

Karen

Leslie,

I can't reach you. Do you get my e-mails?

Karen

Dear Leslie,

I was so relieved when you called this morning. Yes, yes, of course things always appear worse on TV. I know reporters tend to lie on their stomach when taking the pictures, to make the waves look more menacing, but still . . . I'm so glad only a small part of the store roof was damaged. But how annoying that you now have two building sites around you! Ask Rob to fix it; he can certainly move you forward, so you won't have to live with the plastic tarps for long.

Do you want to move into my trailer? I should have offered it earlier—how stupid of me! A trailer, even my small one, has a lot of advantages. Very firm roof, not given to sudden flying-off sessions, for example.

Over here, the weather is picture-perfect. Not a single spring storm in sight. We took the Blackfoot lift today to get to Chief Joseph Bowl, and the snow billowed around our skis like clouds of tiny diamonds. The sky arched above us, blue, blue, blue, so blue, you could lose yourself in it and never return. I felt the wind against my cheeks and my skis gliding through the diamond clouds with the speed that always makes me feel so lithe and light. A wave of happiness surged up in me until it overflowed, and I threw back my head and laughed, thinking I have the most wonderful job on earth. It took me some time to touch ground again. Maybe part of my over-bubbling feelings were connected to the fact that John was close to me all day. I'm getting a little addicted to his presence and am not sure if it is good for me.

Tonight, Terry offered Candy a charging unit for her cell phone. Not a normal charging unit, oh, no, but one she can use in her car. From now on we can call him night and day whenever we end up in dire straits; even if we should forget to charge the phone the night before.

Am not quite sure what he wants to do if the contingency arises, being holed up himself at some godforsaken lake or other, but it pleased both her and him.

I expect Terry to bring in sacks of dried food any day now, in case we get lost on a road with no McDonald's in sight.

Even Columbus himself wasn't as well prepared for his big trip as we are! I teased him a bit, but he only shrugged in his good-natured way and said, "Better safe than sorry."

I have a murky feeling I should mind him.

Instead, as if I didn't know better, and as if I didn't get enough exercise during the day, I asked John and Gerry if they wanted to take an evening walk with me. I met them in the mudroom by chance. That room is getting dearer and dearer to me all the time.

And you don't need to snicker, Leslie, the meeting wasn't contrived at all. I decided that my skis needed a good cleaning and waxing and therefore spent more than an hour there. So you see, it was pure coincidence. Almost.

Gerry looked horrified by the idea and said he preferred TV, upon which unequivocal statement he took himself off, making a detour via the kitchen, where he will diminish the M&M's reserves at an alarming rate, I'm sure. All under the approving eye of a besotted Candy.

But John said he would like a walk, and so we put on our furry walking boots and strolled out. I'm addicted to that crunching noise my boots make when walking in the snow. Our breath formed white clouds in front of our faces, but I was as warm as toast with my thick gloves and woolen cap. Though I did think for a moment that it's easier to look enticing in summer clothes than dressed as a sort of polar bear.

The moonlight glistened on every single snow crystal until I felt the world was an enchanted place and anything was possible. We didn't talk much. I led him past the tennis courts, white and forsaken, then up Nature Trail. The snow deepened there, and at some point John took my gloved hand, and we toiled on until we got to a clearing in the wood and could catch a glimpse of the valley.

Teton Valley slept pure and white, as if nothing bad could ever happen there. We could make out the windows of the guesthouse, like squares of gold against the dark shape of the house. Starting from the drive of the guesthouse, street lamps appeared in regular dots all along the twisting road until they merged into the bright lights of the Village Plaza and Shops.

But it was all below us. Up here, the world was quiet and cold and set apart. The sky stretched over the sharp edges of the mountains, ablaze with stars that twinkled as if a breeze gave them a nudge from time to time.

Not long before, a rabbit had crossed our trail, leaving its shadowed prints in the glistening snow. If it had returned from behind the firs and bidden us a grave good-night, I wouldn't have batted an eyelash. Magic spun its silvery threads around me, and all I could do was look and look and soak it all up. I think it must have shown in my face, because John suddenly said, "It's easy to make you happy, Karen."

"Is it?"

"Yes. You have a special gift, you know that?"

"Have I? Tell me all about it. It sounds nice."

"I've been watching you, and your face lights up so often during the day. Whenever you scan the sky, for example."

"That's because I'm addicted to blue," I said.

"Whenever you glide through the snow too."

I shrugged and laughed. "That's normal."

"Is it? Rowland doesn't look anywhere near that happy when skiing. Nor does Minnie."

"Oh."

"Whenever somebody says something silly. Then your eyes light up, though your mouth remains serious."

"And you say it's a gift?" I finally asked, after I had regained some sort of control over my voice.

"It's a gift to take delight in the small things, isn't it?"

I didn't dare to glimpse at him. To lighten the mood (need I repeat that flirting is not my forte?), I turned back the way we had come and said, "You make me sound like a nice person."

He laughed, falling in with me. "And aren't you?"

"Well. It depends. Put the Turtle close to me, and you'll get a different opinion."

John took my arm and turned me around so I had to face him. "Karen."

"Yes?"

"I have an uneasy feeling about Howard."

I shrugged. "There are always a few bad ones among the raisins. But it's just three weeks every season, so I can manage." I continued to descend.

"Three weeks?"

"Yep. He'll stay a week longer than you will."

"Humph." The snort made it clear. Mr. John Bernett wasn't pleased.

"John, listen."

I must have sounded dead serious all of a sudden, because he threw me a startled glance and said, "I'm listening."

"You don't have to protect me. I'm a grown woman, and I've handled similar situations before."

He took a deep breath, but after a moment he slowly said, "Right."

I was so glad he didn't say anything horrible like, "I like a woman with spunk," so I smiled, and we crunched our way home in companionable silence.

Candy came out of the garage just as we returned and raised her eyebrows when she heard that I had felt the need to go for a walk after several hours on my skis. But I didn't feel like explaining, and so I whisked out my felt slippers and hobbled up the stairs before she could probe into matters I didn't wish to discuss.

Good night.

Karen

Dear Karen,

I've moved into your trailer, but I can tell already I won't stay long. It's suffocating me. How on earth do you stand living in such a tiny space? Sorry, I don't want to offend you, but I had no idea how SMALL it is.

When I read your e-mails, I have a feeling that something far more serious than you wanted is developing here—you know that, don't you? I fear for your heart. Couldn't you flirt a little and have fun for a few weeks, then move on? I'm just so worried that you'll be hurt. After Rob, you said you should have known that your need for independence is much stronger than your need for a partner. You see, I listened to you. And I think you were right.

Sorry to sound so worried—I know it's not like me— but all these building sites with their dust and noise are getting on my nerves. I'm counting the days until the kitchen is done.

Leslie

Dear Leslie,

I'm not offended that you can't live in my trailer. I know it's just me and this thing I have of feeling cozy and well protected if I live in a tiny space. Maybe it's okay because I'm always outside during the day. At least in winter . . . You see, I can't imagine living in a large house. I'd feel all lonely and lost, rattling around the place like a pebble in a shoebox.

I keep my fingers crossed that the work will soon be done! I know how much you hate dust, and I feel for you. . . .

I have to tell you that something new happened today, something bad.

The management of the Teton Valley Ski Tours has a maddening belief that if they spoil your day, they should do it early in the morning. So when I came down for breakfast, as usual with half-closed eyes, I discovered a letter on my plate just in time to avoid biting into it. After my first cup of coffee, I even managed to open it.

When I finished reading it, I was wide awake, something that has never happened at this hour before, and I do hope it will never happen again.

I copy it out for you in all its glory, so you can throw something against the wall in fury (but please don't take my favorite mug).

Dear Ms. Larsen,

We regret to inform you that we have received claims from your current ski group about your behavior. In particular, we have been told that you are carrying on an affair with one member of the group, neglecting the others in consequence. We were also told that you have fallen asleep during lunch breaks and that your style of teaching recalls a "failed attempt at a Charlie Chaplin movie."

We have already discussed previous cases where members of your groups weren't satisfied, and we have to tell you that in case of further claims, we will be forced to act upon them.

Yours sincerely,
Carl Feeder, Manager

I have never been so angry in my whole life. For a second, something red-hot came down in front of my eyes, and a rushing sound exploded in my ears, and I believe that if Howard had been close at that instant, I would not have been responsible for my actions, and you would have to organize that attorney at top speed now.

Luckily, for me and him, he eats his breakfast an hour earlier than I do.

When I glanced up, two pairs of gray eyes were fixed on me, looking as if I was about to die at any second. I might have gone a trifle pale.

"God, what was in that letter?" Gerry blurted out.

I know I shouldn't have given it to them.

First, I should have taken a deep breath and thought about it, and then I should have decided upon a sensible course of action. Most of all, I should have kept all members of the group out of it, as they have a right to a happy holiday. But I was so mad, I didn't stop to think.

When they finished reading, Gerry said, "But who are you having an affair with?" And then he blushed to the roots of his hair and stuttered, "I'm sorry, I shouldn't . . ."

John knew. He met my eyes with a mixture of anger and remorse, and I said, "It's not your fault."

Gerry's eyes grew wide. They jumped from me to his dad and back, and I could tell his mind was racing.

"What can we do?" John asked. And in spite of it all, I felt something warm inside me. He had said *we.*

Gerry stuffed a piece of toast into his mouth. "We'll go there and tell them they're stupid! We'll tell them you're the best ski teacher ever, and that the Turtle is a complete jerk!"

John gave me a lopsided smile. "I'm afraid that won't help," he said.

"Why not? Are you afraid of them?"

His father contemplated him. "No. I'm not afraid. But they'll think I'm biased, and so my statement won't count."

Gerry digested this, and all through the rest of the meal he discussed different ways to punish the Turtle. It was pretty bloody, and I thoroughly enjoyed it, but all too soon we had to leave for class.

I had a terrible morning, thinking all the time about the Charlie Chaplin comparison, and in order to avoid being like him, I turned all stiff and strange, and I could tell that the rest of the group was puzzled.

Isn't it horrible how other people can cramp your style? It shouldn't matter, and yet . . . Howard seemed to enjoy himself. I had to pull myself together to talk to him without hot fury showing in my face and my every word.

The worst was the insinuation about the affair. It was such a clever move. He knew John would have come to my rescue, and efficiently too, so to avoid it, he'd nailed him down with that invented tale.

I hardly dared to glance at John all day for fear anybody would say we were "intimate." Horrible.

And that's just what Howard wants. He manipulates us, and he's succeeding so well. By rights he should leave black marks on the snow wherever he moves, because he's got such a dirty mind.

I mulled over it all day until suddenly I had an idea. Even if John couldn't give his opinion, others could. And I would make them tell management!

I didn't have a chance to tell John during the day, and in the evening he vanished somewhere. So I sat on my bed with my laptop, crossed my legs, and started a questionnaire that would Help the Teton Valley Ski Tours Get Even Better. It would be anonymous, and I would give a copy to every member of my group to fill in tomorrow at lunchtime.

I was just finishing it, with hot cheeks, when a knock came on the door, and as soon as I called out in answer, John poked his head in. "Am I disturbing you?"

"Not at all," I said. "In fact, you can help me. Come here and read this, and tell me what you think."

When we were side by side, I could smell his aftershave and feel his shoulder touching mine. Suddenly I realized how dangerous it was. Exhilarating too. I admit, I wasn't quite myself, pushed high by anger and enthusiasm for my plan.

He read it and grinned. "Fantastic."

And then his eyes met mine, and I swear I would have kept my cool if only he didn't have those dimples. As it was, my hand rose all by itself, and I touched his cheek. I think I wanted to say something—loads of words tumbled through my mind, but they all got stuck, and nothing came out.

He caught my hand and turned it and kissed the inside.

As his lips touched my skin, my heart made a somersault, as if it wanted to catapult itself outside my body, and all those words inside my head fled, and I just stared at him.

Leslie, I can't begin to tell you how I felt. It seems impossible to feel so many contradicting emotions at the same time. I wanted him to continue, to pull me close, and to kiss me. At the same time, I was scared stiff. I wanted to keep my distance, to keep my independence, to stay secure where I know my way.

I can already hear you say, "So what's a kiss? Enjoy it. Go for it."

But I can't.

To me, a kiss is a pledge, a surrender, a promise. I believe I was born a hundred years too late. But I can't change myself. I can't kiss a man just for the fun of it. Embarrassing, really.

I have no clue what he read in my eyes. Maybe I looked like a rabbit in front of a snake?

And then the decision was taken out of our hands—I should

say his hands, because I wasn't about to decide anything—by Candy shouting up the stairs, "Karen, did you want the packed lunch for your group tomorrow or the day after tomorrow?"

I jumped up and ran to the top of the stairs to reply. And when I came back, the moment was gone. John left soon afterward, and I cursed myself for feeling lonely.

Think of me, Leslie.

Karen

Dear Karen,

I can't believe Carl Feeder puts any trust in Howard's judgment. He must be so stupid if he can't see what kind of guy he is. Then again, maybe you're right, and he's only looking for an excuse to fire you. Do be careful. And tell me the sequel! I'm biting my nails here.

Leslie

P.S. Need I repeat that you should lighten up? Nothing has happened, not even a kiss. So take it easy. You need some fun, girl!

P.P.S. Enclosed, you'll find the last turnover sheet. Cool, eh?

Chapter Four

Dear Leslie,

Here's the "sequel," as you named it: It all worked out exactly as planned. The group accepted the questionnaires like lambs and filled them out with much concentration. I went around to collect them afterward. As I held out my hand to get the one from Howard (wishing I could throw it away immediately, but I had already resolved myself that I would stand firm against the temptation), he stared at me and said, "Why should I give it to you?"

I raised my eyebrows. "So I can pass it on to management."

He shook his head with the reptilian movement that gives me the shivers and said in a voice loud enough for all the group to hear, "No. It doesn't make sense to fill out a questionnaire that will be passed on by the only person who's interested in the results."

I could feel myself going red. That slimy toad. How dare he insinuate . . . !

My hand cramped itself around the questionnaires I had already collected. My precious questionnaires! Between my fury and shock, I was unable to say anything. I heard Minnie giggling in a nervous way, and suddenly Gerry started forward with raised fists, muttering something unrepeatable. I put myself into his way and tried to stop him with a glare, wishing fervently John would come. But he had left the terrace after handing me his questionnaire and was nowhere to be seen. All at once, I knew what to do.

"I see your point," I said to the Turtle, and I faked a smile that should have made him feel sick. "Why don't you and Rowland take the questionnaires together to the management office? Does that solution alleviate your fears?" I hope my voice dripped with sarcasm. From the corner of my eye I could see Rowland blinking in surprise at this sudden job.

But the Turtle was a match for me. "There's no need to ask Rowland too," he answered with a smile just as fake as mine. "I can do it myself."

I continued grinning, though it hurt my cheek muscles. If only I could push him down the hill. I didn't want him to be alone with my precious questionnaires for one single minute. "Ah, but you see, Howard, I would prefer if you did it together with Rowland."

Rowland sucked in his breath with surprise, and Minnie's eyes grew large, her gaze jumping from one to the other. Gerry looked as if he wanted to box me down in order to have a go at the Turtle, and it took all my self-control not to step out of his way. (I'm such a good person. I hope the angels noticed it and gave me top credits, to chalk up against the bad-hair days).

"I will give them to management," Rowland suddenly said, and he held out his hand. "No need for you to come too, Howard."

I wanted to hug him. Instead, I passed him the questionnaires. The Turtle, after looking daggers at me, handed over his sheet of wickedness as well. I was so relieved.

And seething. Because now I haven't gotten a chance to skim through the questionnaires, and I have NO clue what they wrote. It is just possible that I have given management a solid base to finally hand me my notice.

Darn, darn, darn.

A minute later, a thought seared through me like liquid fire. Management had no clue they would be getting the questionnaires! Rowland would go to the office and hand them the pile, and they would throw a careless glance at it and tell him they didn't want it!

Immediately I got hold of Rowland and told him to give the papers to Carl Feeder personally, and as soon as the group was out of earshot, I whipped out my cell phone and called Carl, explaining that I had done a little questionnaire in order to get broader feedback about my performance than just one letter. (I made sure my voice was nonchalant and professional).

Carl didn't sound as if he was amused by my idea, but I cut him short by saying that a member of my group was already on the way and that he should make sure to ask him how much chance I had had to change the results. (At this point, my voice did get a trifle sarcastic, I admit).

When I hung up, I thought back to the great times I'd had with the old management team, and I wondered why Carl disliked me so much. Though it's mutual, I admit. Why is it that some people make your hair stand on end the minute they enter a room? I can't seem to behave in a normal way around him; I always get bristly like an old thistle. No wonder he thinks I'm more of a liability than an asset if I behave like that with our guests.

I'm so glad at least the other half of my life is safe and stable, Leslie, with a repaired roof and all. And I barely trusted my eyes when you sent me the last turnover! With the storm and rain these last weeks, I expected something rather dismal.

It's amazing that such a significant increase was due to the change of our Web site. It really has paid off, hasn't it? Uncork a bottle of wine for me, and let's make sure to celebrate together when I'm back! I'll do my special king-prawn skewers for you, and we'll have one of our long summer barbecue nights. When I look through the window at the glistening snow, I can hardly imagine that I will sit outside in shorts in a few months again.

Karen

> *Way to go, Karen! Don't you worry about the content of the questionnaires; you'll be fine.*
>
> *Leslie*

Dear Leslie,

John and Gerry took me out to Chez Martine tonight.

At first I hesitated to accept the invitation, but then I thought I was not going to change my life only because of the Turtle's dirty mind. After all, everybody but Howard knows it's difficult to start an affair under the avid eyes of a fourteen-year-old! So I said, "I'd love to come," just as my pause was becoming a tad too long.

I think John knew why I hesitated (he's getting better and better at this soul-seeing). He smiled but did not say anything.

Do you want to know what I had?

We started with a creamy zucchini soup sprinkled with croutons and a dollop of sour cream. I wanted a second helping but restrained myself, knowing there were other delights in store.

Next came toasted baguette with thick slices of avocado, a bit of lime, and fresh crabs. By then I was already on cloud nine, thinking paradise was somewhere just around the corner.

As main dish, I chose pink-rose Barbary duck breast that melted in my mouth, together with Vichy carrots and potato croquettes and a rich orange sauce that mingled a fruity note amid the duck gravy. I could get addicted to that sweet-and-sour combination.

Dessert was to die for. I chose a kind of hot chocolate muffin, but juicier and richer than normal muffins. And when I dipped my spoon into it, molten Valrhona chocolate oozed out, a bittersweet kind, too hot to lick but, combined with the Bourbon-vanilla ice cream and the star fruit on the side, it was . . . well . . . indescribable. I closed my eyes and savored the taste until even my small toe tingled with pleasure.

John chose a Spanish wine, a Rioja Grand Reserve called Baron de Ley (I asked him to write it down for me), and I tell you, Leslie, up to then I always thought it a bit affected to discuss wine in poetic terms, as if you were describing a collection of trees and spices with several flowers thrown in, but I changed my mind. Immediately. Won't submit you to one of those descriptions now, so don't worry. But I'll buy a bottle one day for a special occasion and share it with you, and then you'll see that I'm right.

What a great piece of luck that Martine agreed to leave France and stay with her husband forever in Teton Valley. She lifted it to unforeseen culinary heights. I think when I'm old and toothless and sit down to my fifty-fifth dish of mashed potatoes in just as many days, I will still remember this evening.

Though it was more than the food. Carl Feeder had taken all of us at Teton Valley Ski Tours to Chez Martine for our Christmas party, and I remember vividly some of the food getting stuck in my throat. But of course I was seated next to him and felt as if I was glued onto a hot plate, simmering softly until done.

Not this time. We laughed so much and discussed everything under the sun. About ways to judge performances of employees, about my preference for carrots and John's enthusiasm for corn, while Gerry loves peas, about the way you see things differently when you get older, about my cross-country trip and tequila in Mexico, about carpets in bookstores and gluing them down, about having to fight so much in life, about jazz music versus classical, and about ski boots being a punishment if they're the wrong make.

It's funny how an expression in the eyes of the person opposite you can make you glow and make you think you're beautiful and witty. It's scary too.

I might be repeating myself, but tell me, how many people can you really talk to? Talk to without restraint, just think out loud?

We parted in the mudroom, hanging our jackets on the appropriate hooks like the good kids we are. Gerry had already shuffled upstairs in his slippers, and John was about to follow, but I held him back, very sexy in my own felt shoes.

"Thank you, John." I wanted to say much more, how I'd never had a comparable dinner, and how I would always treasure the memory, but it all seemed so stilted and clichéd that nothing came out.

And because all those words got stuck, and because it felt wrong to stretch out my hand as if we were generals parting after a summit conference, I stood on tiptoe and brushed my lips across his cheek. When I smelled his skin and felt him so close, my knees decided to start a pudding act, just for a fraction of a second . . . and that proved to be my undoing. I lost my footing in those darn felt things and tumbled against him like a baby elephant trying its first little skip.

He caught me but couldn't keep his own balance; he stepped back and fell in turn, with me on top, onto a conveniently placed bench. An almighty crash rattled the walls, and I thought the house would come tumbling down on top of us.

Gerry rushed through the door. "What happened?"

John hauled me to my feet, smiled down at me, and said, "Unfortunately, nothing."

And that was that.

Now I'm sitting on my bed with a heavy heart. The day after tomorrow is their last day, and then they'll disappear into the Pacific Northwest, and maybe they'll send an e-mail or two, and then it will peter out.

I just hope my feelings will do so too. Yes, you are right. I admit it. I'm getting out of my realm, and it scares me.

I might even be without a job by then. But no, I don't really believe it. The season will end in another three weeks, and though the Easter rush will soon be over, I'm sure they won't kick me out before that. After all, I'm not exactly doing damage to their business. At least, I hope they see it that way.

But they might hand me my notice. I'll try not to think of it. I love Teton Valley so much. A gypsy with roots, after all. It's quite a new experience.

Good night, Leslie. Sleep well.

Karen

Dear Karen,

They won't fire you. You're the best ski instructor in the valley, and even if Carl Feeder doesn't know it, everybody will tell him. So don't you worry.

Steel yourself for the good-bye. From all you write, it sounds as if John is a great man. Sigh. Why can't he live in the Hamptons?

Have to go—there's dust on every single book in the store. BTW, I'm enclosing a picture of a new wall storage system. I think it would be ideal for the wall in the back, so we could finally replace the crooked table there, and the price seems reasonable. I would like them to be white, not black, though. They come in both colors. What do you think?

Leslie

Dear Leslie,

You won't believe what happened today! I stumbled into the house this afternoon, still in my heavy boots, and had just started to take them off when Candy crept in and closed the door with a soft click behind her. Usually she's the loudest person I know, shouting and banging doors and whatever, so I was startled. "What's the matter, Candy?" I asked. "Do we have a murderer in the house?"

She shook her head and sank beside me onto the bench. "Karen," she whispered. "It's Howard."

I felt a surge of anger. "What on earth has he been doing now?"

She stared at me. "He's not done anything. He's sitting in the kitchen, crying."

Get that, Leslie! My mouth fell open. "He's doing what?"

"Shh, not so loud. He's crying."

"What on earth is he crying for? Don't tell me he repents having made my life a misery."

Her eyes grew large. "Has he done that?"

"He sure has."

"Well." She seemed at a loss and stared at her hands. "No, no, he has not repented. He's sad."

"Humph. Don't ask me to feel bad for him."

"But he's crying because of you!"

At this point, I thought I was having a bad dream. "Because of me?"

"Shh! Lower your voice! Yes, because of you. He said he was in love with you, and last year, when he spent two weeks at Teton Valley, you encouraged him. . . ."

I jumped up. "I did what?"

"Karen! Stop shouting! That's what he said, and—"

"He's suffering from delusions! Maybe you should check him for drugs. Cocaine, probably. Isn't that the stuff that makes the world pink and green?"

"I don't know, and I don't care," Candy hissed, "but I'm sorry for him because he's devastated. He says you prefer John now, who's hanging around you all the time, and all at once you're pretending you never felt anything for him!"

"I'm not pretending anything at all." I had trouble keeping my voice down. "I didn't like him last year, and this year I like him even less. He's a turtle." I wondered if steam was coming out of my ears by now. It sure felt like it.

"He just looks like one!"

"Never mind. Why are you telling me this elevating story?"

Candy stared at me. "I didn't know you could be so sarcastic."

"Well, he has done his best to shred my reputation with management, in particular Carl, who was all too ready to believe him, so I really don't know why I should be nice about it."

"Oh." She chewed the inside of her cheek. "Could it be that he was only trying to get your attention?"

I shrugged. "I would have preferred flowers." Then I brought myself up short. I know Candy; she's much too softhearted for her own good. "But please don't feel obliged to make him feel better by giving him free extra days to stay. If you do, I'll move to the Jolly Time hotel."

Candy grinned. "As if I would."

Phew.

But later, I had to think about Howard. Isn't it strange how some people come to be so twisted, Leslie? Maybe I should feel sorry for him. Maybe I will—at some point in the future, when the letter from management has stopped smarting.

Sometimes life is too complicated for me.

Karen

P.S. I don't want to think about tomorrow. It's John's last day. We'll do one farewell descent, and that's it. It's a nice one, though. We'll take the Sacajawea lift to Peaked Mountain. I've saved it for last to make it a wonderful exclamation point at the end of their holiday.

And then, the next morning, they will leave with the shuttle to the Jackson Hole airport. It doesn't bear thinking about. I've done it so often, and it has never been like this. You're so right: I should steel myself. But how exactly do I manage that?

P.P.S. The new shelf system looks good to me! I like the idea that we can change the distance between the shelves as needed. White is perfect too. We can always paint the walls if we want a new color scheme.

Dear Karen,

No excuse for the Turtle! Don't take things too seriously. If he wants you to like him, he could start with something revolutionary . . . like being kind to you.

Matthew came to the store today, all smiles and smirks. I can't believe I ever fell for him. I threw him out. It was great fun. You should have seen Mrs. Bluebottle's face. She was fascinated.

Have to fall into bed now. Rob wants to discuss something about the floor with me tomorrow at 7:00 A.M. Later, he's booked. Ugh.

Leslie

Dear Leslie,

I didn't think you'd still be awake at this time! I love it when I get an instant reply. Makes me feel so close to you, knowing you're right in front of your computer, just as I am.

I'm glad to hear you threw Matthew out of the store today. You should have pushed him a bit farther, down the pier, to cool him off. He deserves it, after the heartbreak he put you through last year.

Way to go!
Karen

Thx, dear friend. Snore. Am half-asleep already. Good night.

Leslie

Dear Leslie,

The world has turned upside down.

It all started so well. The sun came up with a glorious halo of red just as we were swinging upward in the Sacajawea lift. Yes, we made an early start, and yes, getting up was torture. But it's worth it (as long as it doesn't become a habit)!

When the sun touched the snowy peaks, they came alive, softly at first, with a dark lilac that later slid down to pool in the shadows. Then the light became fierce and red and strong, taking your breath away; next, the mountains lightened until they were all rose and pink, like something out of a children's fairy-tale book, and finally everything burst into crystal light, and all the slopes glittered and twinkled.

I can't talk when I see a sunrise in the mountains.

The only thing I can do is drink it all in and feed my soul.

That's not a cliché, I can actually feel how my innermost being (wherever it may be) soaks up the beauty, and it's exactly the feeling you have when physical hunger is stilled.

You know what I particularly love about a snowy landscape?

The forms. There are no rough edges, no sharp angles; everything is smoothed, softened, as if a benevolent hand had caressed it. I always wish I could fly over it and follow the soft curves with my hand, blowing up dancing clouds of snow in passing with my breath.

I was still bewitched by the beauty when we got to the top of the slope, and so I faced my group and said: "This is our last trip together, and I want you to enjoy it to the fullest. Don't worry about your technique; don't worry about being slow or fast. Just glide through the snow, and drink it all in, so it may remain a memory until you can come back."

I smiled at them all, faced the trail, and pushed myself off with my ski poles, making the little crunching sound that's so exhilarating.

But for no reason at all, there were suddenly tears in my eyes, so I slowed down and let the others overtake me.

When we were about halfway down, the group had spread out, but I could see them all. Gerry was somewhere in the front, together with Rowland; next came Minnie with Howard and most of the others; and I dawdled behind, making sure we left no one on the mountain by mistake. John was by my side. "Why don't you race on ahead?" I shouted. "Feel the speed."

He shook his head with that devastating smile of his. "Because I prefer to be here."

Right. I turned back to the slope, and that was when it happened.

Gerry, only visible as a tiny figure on the slope below, must have hit an icy patch. His feet splayed out, he lost his balance, and then he crashed down, and his speed catapulted him right down the slope in a flurry of arms and legs and red woolly cap.

I heard John taking in his breath with a sharp sound that cut right through me.

Next thing I knew, I shot down the slope, overtaking all the others who stood frozen in place, horrified, until I finally dropped to my knees beside Gerry.

"Gerry."

His face was white, the freckles showing like a spattering of dark brown ink. Those thick lashes lay like feathers on his cheeks.

"Gerry!"

He opened his eyes, and the pain in them made me wince. "My leg." His voice sounded so different, weak and traumatized.

I checked his legs. The left one lay twisted at an angle that hurt just to look at, and his trousers were torn from the fall, right above the knee.

I took off his ski boot, trying to move his legs as little as possible, but I knew it was torture.

In the meantime John arrived and knelt at the other end, holding Gerry's head. I glanced at John's face once, but the feelings in it were so raw, I immediately averted my gaze.

The rest of the group stood around us, mute and helpless.

Then I saw it. Something dark oozed through the gap in Gerry's trousers. My blood congealed. I felt like an icicle, Leslie, dead to all feeling, unable to move. Thank God, my training kicked in at that point, and I sort of went on autopilot. I fixed John's belt above the wound to stop the blood, hating the look on Gerry's white face, made Rowland call a helicopter, and gave Gerry something to drink.

We had to wait till June before the helicopter finally arrived— or so it felt. I couldn't look at John's face; all the emotion there was too much to bear.

Gerry was still conscious by the time the helicopter arrived. There's nothing to distract a fourteen-year-old from pain like being flown away in a helicopter.

But John looked as if someone had kicked him in the face when they told him he couldn't ride in the helicopter, as there wasn't enough room.

I grabbed his arm. "I'll take you to Valley Hospital," I said. "We'll be there in no time at all. I promise."

As soon as the helicopter had flapped away with its deafening noise, shaking the trees with an angry hand, I gave Rowland responsibility for the group, asked them to report to Steve at the Guest Check-In, plastered a fake smile onto my face, fixed my skis back on, made a tight arch, and nodded at John, who was already standing ready for takeoff, taut as a wire.

Off we raced.

Have you ever skied for your life, Leslie?

That's how it felt. We rushed down at a speed that cut the breath off our mouths and made the wind hammer at us with iron fists. We were going side by side, but at one point John swerved to the side, overtaking me. "John!" I yelled and pulled to a stop.

I could see he hated to curb the speed, but he did.

"That's no good," I panted. "Stay beside me. It's fast enough as it is. I don't want both my men with broken limbs on my hands."

"But I . . ."

"No."

He took a deep breath, and I could see the fierce struggle inside him reflected on his face. Finally he said, "All right."

I nodded and pushed off again, keeping the speed at the top limit, toeing the line of being irresponsible. It scared me, but I found it exhilarating too, though I was ashamed to feel like that, and I wouldn't admit it to anybody but you, Leslie.

When we finally arrived at the valley, I was gasping for breath, soaked through with sweat. We jumped off our skis and ran to the guesthouse, where we threw the skis helter-skelter into the mudroom.

Five minutes later we had packed all that was needed, I had given Candy hasty instructions and borrowed her car, and then we were off. The drive only took about twenty minutes, but it seemed never-ending. I was so afraid that Gerry had been seriously injured and kept asking myself if I could have prevented it somehow, but I tried to push that thought away. I couldn't have known about that bit of ice. Then I remembered that I had managed to put on a new T-shirt and packed a large one for John because I guessed he would not have taken the time to get rid of his sweat-soaked one. When I told him to put it on, he stared at me.

"You're amazing."

I liked the tone of his voice. He almost sounded like the normal John again.

"You want me to bare my chest in a car in the middle of winter?"

"Well, it won't be bare for long, and I've turned the heat to its maximum," I replied, "so stop behaving as if I asked you to take off all your clothes."

He grinned, and then he said, in a curious voice, "You know something, Karen?"

"What?"

"You can ask me anything you want."

It sounded darn serious, and suddenly my ears felt hot, and I'm sure they turned flaming red. But instead of laughing and returning an easy answer, as you would have done, I fell silent and didn't say another word for the rest of the journey, keeping my gaze fixed on the road while he pulled on my biggest black T-shirt, which was much too small for him.

Our arrival at the hospital was a nightmare. The receptionist was precise and correct and had all the time in the world. He asked John to fill in and sign about twenty-seven forms, and still we had no clue how Gerry was. The man kept saying he would check but never managed to do so.

Finally some nurse whisked by and said they were operating on Gerry right then, and we would get news when they were done. I pulled John into one of the waiting-room seats. Then I rummaged in my bag, an excellent excuse not to look at the tight line of his clenched jaw. "Want some M&M's?"

He took a handful like a man in a trance, and I searched my brain for something clever and appropriate to say.

Nothing.

All day long I can talk like a parrot, but the one moment I really need it, everything dries up within me, and I sit mute and stupid, not being any help at all.

I chewed my lip for a while while John stared straight ahead with strained eyes.

Finally I figured that talking about Gerry would help him and not seem too obvious a change of subject. So I said, "Has Gerry talked about that music school in the last few days?"

"No. We've shelved that subject for the vacation."

"You know, you're real lucky with Gerry. Other teenagers would make your life miserable."

"Well, we're in a kind of probation period; I guess that's why I'm being spared the teenager fits."

I had no clue what he was talking about. "Probation?"

John stared into the distance. "He'd been living with his mother until August. But since they weren't getting along, he asked if he could come and stay with me. So we've been living together for just eight months."

"So that's why!" I told you their relationship was unusual.

That got his attention, and he looked at me for the first time since we'd entered that disinfected place. "What do you mean?"

"I noticed he was triumphant to be in your group. And I could tell he enjoyed being with you, as if it was a special treat. That puzzled me."

John sighed. "It's my mistake. You see, I work a lot. Always have. When Gerry came to live with me, I didn't understand that he would want to share more time with me and that working until nine every night wasn't in the cards anymore. He was lonely. And sad. He had expected a different life with me, a sort of male companionship."

He continued by telling me he'd only learned about Gerry's feelings at Christmastime, when Gerry asked him in a shy way if, maybe, they could have more days with time for the two of them together. When John saw how nervous he was, he realized what he was doing. And not for the first time either.

I tried to swallow a lump in my throat. "Not for the first time?"

"Celina, my wife, moved out, leaving a letter, telling me I probably wouldn't notice she was gone, but she wanted to leave some sign anyway."

"Did you fight to get her back?"

He stared at me. "No. The thought never entered my head. In

fact, I . . . I believe I was relieved." His gaze probed my face. "Do I shock you?"

"Yes."

He passed a hand over his face. "I'll try to explain. You see, I had just founded my company. It had been a dream of mine, and it was so exciting to see it grow and to see it happen and to develop new products that were grabbed up by the market."

"Electronics, wasn't it?"

"Yeah. Celina and I met in high school and married right afterward. She wanted to settle, to start a family, to develop roots. I wanted to see the world, to change things."

"I understand," I whispered. Oh, how well I understood.

John explained that, for him, it was a burden to know he was never meeting her expectations, forever late to some social function or family gathering, never mowing the lawn on time, never remembering to call his mother-in-law on her birthday.

I shook my head. "But she should have understood, too, that you had dreams and that you weren't satisfied with the humdrum of daily life."

He took a deep breath. "She couldn't understand that. I don't think she can understand it to this day. To her, the years passing by in a steady rhythm have something soothing to offer her; it gives her stability. It stifles me. And so she left."

"I believe it was you who left first." The words slipped out before I could stop them. Oh, Leslie, I was so scared that he would close up at that point, but he didn't, and I liked him all the more for it.

Instead, he gave me a startled glance, then said slowly, "In a way, yes. Though I wouldn't have admitted it at the time."

"How old was Gerry?"

"Three."

I felt chilled, thinking of little Gerry, but I didn't say anything, couldn't.

"Celina remarried within a year, to a guy who adores her and who is happy washing his car every Saturday."

I threw him a glance. "You despise him."

His gray eyes met mine. "I used to. Am not so sure lately."

"So the life of routine has become more attractive to you?"

"No. But with Gerry I've noticed that my oh-so-broad mind was, in a way, just as narrow as Celina's. I didn't see anything but my work. Maybe I should say my passion—that fits better."

How well I understood that! I asked him what he did to change things, after that day at Christmas, and he told me they had chosen the Teton holiday after three evenings of careful discussion. He said it was fun and that he had promised Gerry to turn off his cell phone during vacation, with the exception of one hour after dinner.

"And how does it feel?"

"Odd."

"Have you cut down your work hours too?"

He sighed. "I tried to. But it's hard. A little bit of passion sounds like a contradiction in itself, doesn't it?"

I grinned at him. "It does."

And then something strange happened. Our eyes locked, and the smile fled from his eyes. In an instant the air between us got charged with electricity, and I had trouble with my breathing, feeling wonderful and shaken at the same time.

I was scared of the magnitude I could glimpse behind it all and knew I had to say something, anything, to dissolve the tension. Taking a deep breath, I grabbed the bag in my lap and said with a squeaky voice, "Want some M&M's?"

At that instant a thin man in a white coat approached in a vague manner, as if he wasn't quite sure where he was and what he wanted to do there anyway. "Mr. Bernett?"

John leaped up, towering over him. "Yes?"

"Will you follow me, please?"

I found I was holding John's hand, though I couldn't tell if I had reached for it. John clasped it in grim determination, and even if I had wanted to, I was unable to free myself.

We sat down in a white room, and the doctor fixed us with mild surprise in his brown eyes, as if he had no clue what we wanted. But then he opened his mouth and poured out a bewildering list of the things that had happened to Gerry's leg. I didn't get much, but the main facts I grasped: It was a clean break, and it would heal with time. He had lost a lot of blood and was weak, but, being young, that wasn't critical. For a minute I felt dizzy with relief and was glad of John's hand keeping me firmly in this world.

"Who put the belt around his leg?" the doctor suddenly asked.

"Karen did." John smiled at me, the strain around his eyes completely gone.

"Well done, Mrs. Bernett." The doctor's gaze shifted around the room, as if he was looking for a little orientation to what this was all about. "Few mothers have that presence of mind when an accident happens."

I opened my mouth, but he had already drifted toward the door in his irresolute way.

"When can we see Gerry?" John asked.

The doctor blinked at his watch, as if he was surprised to find it on his arm. "He should be transferred to his room in about ten minutes, but he'll still be groggy. It's room 236."

And the next minute we stood outside the door in the white hallway and stared at each other with crooked grins on our faces.

Finally I swallowed, held up the little bag I still clutched in my free hand, and croaked, "Want some M&M's?" and John said, "Oh, Karen," with a voice I barely recognized and took my face in both his hands and kissed me.

Now, don't get me wrong; it wasn't a passionate kiss or something. It's hard to become passionate in a white hospital hallway smelling of disinfectant. It was more the culmination of a crazy day, a crest breaking over, sweeping anxiety and relief, and I think a sort of thank-you-for-everything along with it. I took it in the spirit it was given, being more than a little confused myself and shaking in my shoes.

When we broke away, grinning like idiots, I caught a movement out of the corner of my eye and froze. Who do you think stood next to us, his mouth a prim line of disapproval?

Yes, right on.

Carl. Carl Feeder.

The manager of the Teton Valley Ski Tours in person.

The one who had been told that I was spending too much time with my "affair" instead of concentrating on every member of the group with equal zeal.

The one who would readily believe I was smooching in a hospital hallway while my group had gone lost on the mountain.

I grabbed my voice from out of my stomach and introduced them. And you'll never guess what happened next, Leslie.

John put his arm around my shoulder with ease and pulled me close, saying, "I'm so glad we finally meet, Carl. We've been wanting to tell you for so long, but there never was a chance. Karen and I are engaged." He stifled my gasp by pulling me against his chest. "Have been for months, in fact. And since she couldn't take any time off, I figured I would join her group, so we would see each other a little."

Carl's face looked as if all his muscles had gone stiff. "Congratulations. And when is the great day?" I was sure I heard an ironic note in his voice.

"September seventeenth," John smoothly said over my head.

"I see." The corners of Carl's mouth pinched themselves into little knots.

I hunted for a change of topic. "How come you're here, Carl?"

"I just visited my mother. And you?"

"Haven't you heard about the accident?"

His eyebrows snapped together. An accident is bad publicity. "No. What happened?"

"Gerry, John's son, slipped on an icy patch and broke his leg. We've only just heard that he'll be fine."

"An icy patch? How come you didn't prevent the accident?"

I took a deep breath, but before I could shoot my livelihood to smithereens, John tightened his grip, pulled me along, and threw over his shoulder, "Carl, I'm afraid we have to go. Gerry will be in his room any minute now, and we want to be by his bed. See you soon."

And with that, he propelled me through the door and up the stairs like some sort of bulky luggage.

As soon as the door closed behind us, I whipped around with my fists on my hips and hissed, "Why on earth did you say that? Are you completely out of your mind? I don't want to be engaged to you, even in sham, and I don't want to face all the complications afterward!"

He stared at me as if I had banged an entire wall over his head, but I couldn't stop myself, I was so furious. "Thank you so much, Mr. Bernett. What a high-handed way to solve a problem! 'She's engaged to me,'" I mimicked. "Perfect. And so nobody can hurt me anymore? That's not gonna work! You'll leave in a short time, forgetting all about your chivalrous moment, and I'll be stuck here, facing the crowd, having to tell them the wedding has been called off! Everybody will gape at me, awkward and curious at the same time, whispering about me. Thank you very much! What a great service you did me! I'll look like a complete fool!"

I was so worked up, I couldn't stop myself anymore,

though he tried to get a word in edgewise. "And just why did you think I couldn't work myself out of this on my own? I've told you before, and I'm telling you again: I'm not dependent on some male to help me get my job right. I've solved problems like these in the past, without your precious help!"

He looked horrified, and all at once I came to my senses. John had no way of knowing that Rob had done a similar thing to get me committed all those years ago, and that I hate nothing more than being pushed. You would have known, Leslie, and would have understood. When I realized that, I tried to backpedal. "Gosh, I'm sorry, John. But you've hit a sore spot."

"Yes, I can see that," he said slowly. "I'm sorry. I truly thought it would help."

"Yes, yes." I swiveled around, so I wouldn't have to meet his eyes. I was so ashamed of my outburst. "Let's go and find Gerry, shall we?"

Right in front of Gerry's door, I stopped short. "Maybe you don't want me in there. Why don't you go first?"

He fixed me with his gaze for a second, then nodded and walked in.

I leaned against the wall and stared at the gray linoleum floor, deflated like an old balloon.

Stupid, stupid me. We had been so close. Why did I have to go and destroy it all? Why did I have to get on my high horse and throw a tantrum? He'd meant it for the best. And, worse, I knew it.

But I can't stand high-handed ways. You know how much I hate it when people make decisions for me. I don't want to be protected! I don't want any protective wings above me; I want the sky. Blue and endless.

Well, if I'm perfectly honest, I want that most of the time. There are times, just a few, when I do want to roll up and hide in someone's arms. And if I'm totally honest—more than necessary, in fact—then I have to admit, John would be a good person to run to in such a case. Only I would have to do the running first.

Which I didn't do in this case.

And that's just the problem.

Oh, Leslie, why does life have to be so complicated?

I was still flagellating myself when the door opened, and John looked out with a smile. "Gerry's asking for you."

I shook myself, and, pretending all was fine, I marched into the room. "Well, Gerry, that was a pretty dramatic finale."

He grinned, and it lifted my heart. "They say you saved my life."

"Oh, wow. Dramatic stuff. Do you think I'll get a medal? I want it big and golden."

"I'll tell them." John smiled at me in a cautious way that made me feel as if I was a tamed tiger, quiet in general but subject to sudden dangerous fits.

Gerry didn't notice the strained atmosphere between us. "The helicopter was cool," he said.

"Yeah. You'll have loads to tell your friends when you're back in school."

His face clouded over. "They say I'll have to stay here for a week." Before I could reply, he shot a look at John and said, "Dad doesn't want me to ask you, but I don't see why. You see, he has an important meeting on Monday, but he wants to cancel it and stay here. Only I don't think it's necessary. He can fly home and return after the meeting."

"Seattle isn't around the corner, Gerry." John's voice sounded as if he was being strangled. "If I return home, I'll be gone for two days at least."

Gerry nodded. "Yeah, but I can manage that. I'm not a baby anymore. Besides, Karen will be here."

John frowned. "The meeting isn't that important."

And I bet you don't want to ask any favors of me right now, I thought.

Gerry pushed himself up onto one elbow. "But when we booked the holiday, you said there was no way you could cancel the meeting! You said it had been awful to organize it, with all those people involved and the president of . . ."

"I know I said that." John scowled at his son. "But you had an accident—that's more important."

I contemplated John. Whatever he did right now, he could only lose. If he insisted on staying, Gerry would think he was treating him like a baby. But if he returned to Seattle, Gerry might easily think he didn't care enough, in spite of all his protests. Unless John accepted my help. Which he would not want to do right now.

"Gerry," I said, "are you sure you'll be fine if your dad leaves you here? No need to pretend a stiff upper lip; say what you really think."

"I'll be fine." Gerry didn't hesitate. "Because I know you'll be here. If it wasn't for that, I might feel a bit lonely."

I had to hide a smile. What an admission from a fourteen-year-old! I liked him all the more for it. And I have to admit, it made me feel good, the way he accepted that I would be there when he needed help.

Isn't it crazy, Leslie? In a way, Gerry had commandeered me just as his father had, but in his case, I liked it. I didn't have the time to think about my contorted character, though, because John pierced me with those gray eyes of his and said, his tone dry, "And how do YOU feel about it?"

I have to say, he learns his lessons quickly.

"It's fine with me," I replied.

"Yeah," Gerry cut in. "Because we're friends."

John's eyes held mine. "Are we?"

I swallowed, feeling like jelly. "We are."

When I drove John home through the night, we barely talked.

Things were still strained between us. As we walked through the door of the guesthouse, he suddenly clasped my hand and said, "Thank you, Karen."

I didn't know what to say. Do you know any man who manages to say thank you after having been shouted at?

So I just nodded and hurried to my room. And here I am, writing this much too long e-mail to get it all off my chest. It's a good thing I'm a night owl and don't need much sleep; otherwise, I would have broken down long ago.

Hmm.

There's something I have to admit, Leslie.

Just between you and me.

I think part of my anger was due to the fact that I liked the idea of the engagement much too much. Can you believe that?

I'm scared to death.

Karen

Dear Karen,

Oh, dear. I could tell it would come to that point, but I had been hoping that something would prevent it. You were a trifle unfair to John, but I think you know that. I do understand, though. If only Rob hadn't pushed you into your marriage with that very trick. You should tell John about it, so he'll understand why you overreacted.

Now, where do you go from here? What do you want?

Love,
Leslie

Dear Leslie,

I wished I knew what I want. I can't tell. I'm so confused.

John has gone. It's crazy how empty a place can be when just one person is missing.

The new group has arrived, and they're a well-behaved

bunch. Even Howard seems to have returned to some semi-normal behavior, which is a relief.

Maybe Carl told him I'm engaged to John as opposed to having an "illegitimate affair." Gag. If yes, I have John to thank, but I prefer not to think about it. No, I can't tell John about my history with Rob. If I did, I would insinuate that he really wants to marry me, and I don't believe that for a minute.

I spend my evenings at the hospital and have organized a portable DVD-player for Gerry, so he can watch films of famous jazz concerts during the day.

Sometimes I call John or he calls me, and I tell him about Gerry's progress and about the Turtle. In turn, he tells me about his day. At first we were a bit stiff with each other, but without discussing it we settled back into the comfortable way of talking we had before the incident at the hospital. This afternoon I dared to ask the question I've been wanting to ask all along: Why doesn't Gerry want to stay with his mother any longer? I mean, it's one thing for a teenager to wish his parents to Timbuktu . . . but another to move out, particularly if it's only a move to another parent who's not lax about rules either, if I judge the matter correctly.

"It's because Celina vetoed the music career completely," John said.

"But so have you."

"Not at all," John said. "I haven't yet made up my mind, and until then, he can take music lessons until he drops, as far as I'm concerned. If his other grades don't suffer, that is."

"Did she . . . did she stop his lessons?"

"She planned to."

"But why? Did he play night and day and stop doing his homework?"

John sighed. "No, he managed to do it all. Unfortunately, he made it clear that he would never consider another career, and

Celina panicked and wanted to stop him now before it was too late."

I didn't say anything, but John guessed right.

"I know," he said, "it wasn't exactly diplomatic. On either side. If they had shelved the topic, it would have sorted itself out. Anyway, after a row that ripped off the roof of Celina's house, Gerry came to me and asked me if he could move in. I reeled, but I couldn't and wouldn't say no."

"Didn't Celina resent your taking him?"

"At first she did. But Gerry has the right to choose who he wants to stay with, you know. I tried to make them both calm down. Celina went back on her word and promised that he could continue with his lessons. But it was too late. In the meantime Gerry decided he liked the idea of a male household and refused to budge."

"Stubborn, is he?"

He laughed. "Like his father."

I like to talk to him. We have the same attitude about so many things, the same way of looking at things.

Hmm, I just read the last sentences again. No, they don't get across what I feel. What I mean is, we share the same kind of hunger. A hunger to see more, to learn more. A hunger to move. To go on, all the time. It's a sort of curiosity, mixed with passion for what we do.

Of course, his world is electronics. I always thought there was no better way to send me to sleep than a conversation about electronics. But no, not if John starts to explain it. We should make him write a book about it. It's riveting; it truly is. (Stop laughing.) And it's not because I'm in . . . well, because I like him so much.

But the funny thing is, he says exactly the same thing about me. You see, he never read much. But I told him about a few books I thought he would like, and he bought one and said he enjoyed it. And the things he said proved he did read it, not only the description on the back.

I feel like I know him so well, even though it's only been two and a half weeks. I feel as if I can say anything I want, without fearing censure, and I have the impression it's the same with him too.

But the thing he said at the hospital is coming back to me all the time, haunting me. "A little bit of passion is a contradiction in itself."

It's so true. If you do something one hundred percent, there's not a single percentage left for anything else. And I think that's why I had to split up with Rob at the time. Lately I think a lot about the reasons we didn't match, and it's becoming clearer now. Rob was a passionate vintner and carpenter, rooted deep in local soil. I'm a passionate gypsy. Doesn't work, does it? But does that mean I can only be happy with another gypsy? Sounds ridiculous, doesn't it?

I'm all confused. It's getting late. Maybe tomorrow will help me see more clearly. And the day after tomorrow John will come back. I feel a little thrill deep in my stomach whenever I think about it. But on the other hand, he will take Gerry away. And once they're gone, all my musing about one hundred percent passion will be theory and peter out with time.

It's a good thing Candy and I will leave for our glorious trip soon afterward. It'll take my mind off things, and it's always fun to be with Candy. What good is life if you don't have anything to look forward to? I'll cling to that!

Good night,
Karen

Dear Karen,

I don't get this "one hundred percent passion" thing at all. The way I see it, you have to snatch a bit of happiness everywhere. Don't be so serious about everything. Life is fun if you don't let it control you!

Have I told you my new kitchen is wonderful? The

*floor still smells of pine; it feels strong and reliable be-
neath my feet, and I'm so happy to be back home.*

Leslie

Dear Leslie,

I'm so glad you're back home . . . enjoy your kitchen!

I would love to take things easier, but it seems I'm not cut out for it. Maybe there's some tragic Russian root somewhere in my past. Think Tolstoy. Anyway, I'll work on becoming more easy-going, though I find it hard right now, because something bad happened. Again. My horoscope for this year should have said something like, "If you know someone who dabbles in time travel, make sure you skip this year."

I was visiting Gerry in the hospital, having a spirited discussion about the difference between skiing and snowboarding, when Candy exploded into the room.

I stared at her. Her right arm looked like a rolled-up quilt, all in white, held by a sling. With cheeks like wax instead of her usual cheerful robin-red, she dropped into the visitor's chair next to Gerry's bed as if she had wobbly knees. "Thank God I found you," she panted. "Since you have my car, and Terry has taken his to the garage, I had to ask my mother for a ride, but she couldn't wait. You can give me a lift back."

"What on earth happened to you?"

She told us.

In short, she slipped today on a minuscule patch of water in the kitchen of the guesthouse and managed to break her wrist. It's a complicated thing, and apparently she has to keep her arm still as much as she can. For several weeks. Four to six, maybe even eight—they can't define it any better. So . . . there's no way we can go on our cross-country trip together.

When my brain had assimilated this, my stomach felt as if I had swallowed an icy rock. I wanted to burst into tears.

Of course, I tried to hide my disappointment; after all,

Candy is worse off than I am, and I'm so sorry for her. It must hurt so much. So I fixed on a smile—but I'm afraid I fooled neither her nor Gerry.

I drove Candy home, and we said we would simply postpone it for a year.

But a whole year, Leslie. That's an eternity.

And what am I to do during this April break? I can't go on my own. It wouldn't be any fun at all. And there's no way I can face home. Any of my homes. I want to see something different.

We spent the evening calling everybody who might be able to take over Candy's jobs until the season ends. Then we arranged them into shifts. When Terry returned from the garage, we explained it all to him, and he in turn got on the phone and canceled his fishing trip. Candy tried to make him go anyway, but he flicked her cheek with a finger and said, "I wouldn't have a quiet minute if I knew you'd be here on your own. Don't worry, I'll take you somewhere comfy, poppet, where people will serve you all day long."

I swallowed hard and decided that passionate relationships are overrated.

Have to go to bed now. I hope sleep will make me forget my dire prospects.

Karen

Dear Karen,

Oh, no! How I wish I could help. Why don't you go to a travel agency and book a flight, just any flight, to whatever is on offer? Would that alleviate your gypsy instincts?

Tell me if I can do something!

Leslie

Dear Leslie,

John landed sometime this afternoon, and I thought I would see him in the evening, at the hospital. So I hurried to the guesthouse after having finished the last skiing course, intent on losing as little time as possible. And just as I rounded the corner, I cannoned into a guy standing there, and when I looked up, it was John.

I dropped my skis, and—well, how can I put it?—I'm afraid I threw myself into his arms. Literally. In fact, I think I almost pushed him to the ground, like an oversized puppy.

I'm certain he was just as surprised as I was. Fortunately, he didn't allow me enough time to collect myself and get all red and embarrassed.

Instead, he held me and kissed me.

I've never been kissed like that, Leslie. I forgot who I was and where I was, and everything sort of faded, until there was nothing left but John's lips on mine and his arms holding me close, stopping me from shaking, stopping me from falling or floating, I couldn't say which.

What did I say about the hospital kiss? That it wasn't passionate? Well.

This one was.

And I didn't hold anything back, as if I didn't have any problems with passion-percentages or roots or whatever; I just slipped into the moment and forgot everything.

Finally he released me, and we stared at each other, stunned.

He blinked, then said, "I missed you."

"It was empty here too."

And then he kissed me again, slowly this time, brushing my lips gently, tantalizingly, until I felt like devouring him all in one piece.

At long last I said, "I thought I would only see you at the hospital."

His gray eyes smiled into mine. "I couldn't wait."

"But what did Gerry say?"

"He was about to fall asleep and said it was kind of me to pick you up."

"Kind, eh?"

He grinned. "Very kind."

Later, John took me to the hospital, and though nothing at all had changed, I felt great, sort of floaty and light. Beautiful too. Isn't it strange what a difference one person can make?

As soon as I said hello to Gerry, he said, "Have you told her, Dad?"

"No."

"Told me what?" I asked.

Gerry almost jumped up and down on his bed with enthusiasm, bandaged leg and all. "I told Dad about Candy's arm and how sad you were that you couldn't go on your cross-country trip, and we thought we would invite you to come and stay with us."

I shot a look at John. He had that she-might-turn-into-a-tiger-again expression on his face, a little doubtful, not sure how I would react.

"I . . . um. That's very kind," I said. My head whirled. It was all a bit quick.

Yesterday I thought I would be saying good-bye to them, and now here I am, kissed and invited.

"Seattle is great," Gerry continued. "I'll have to go to school, though, but we could spend the evenings together and the weekends, and maybe Dad can take off a day or so." This was accompanied by a doubtful look to his father. "Anyway, there's loads to do and see. We've got the zoo and the Seahawks stadium and . . ."

Seattle. In April. Oh, my God. It will be muddy and rainy.

On the other hand, it means being with John. I swallowed.

"Why don't you think about it?" John cut in. "There's enough time, and we thought it might compensate a bit for the loss of your trip."

I met his gaze, and suddenly I knew that if I went there, it'd be more than just a few days of vacation. And I'm not ready for that. I felt as if someone had slipped a carpet from beneath my feet; everything was moving too quickly. "Yes," I slowly said. "I'll think about it. Thank you for the invitation."

Gerry looked crestfallen. He must have imagined me jumping sky-high, but then, he doesn't know about my complicated scruples, not to mention the mud memories that are inextricably linked to Seattle.

I couldn't hold on to myself; I gave him a quick hug. He returned it in an awkward way, but he couldn't make head nor tails of me, it was plain to see.

His father can, though. Much more than feels comfortable to me. It's not always easy to watch someone reading your thoughts.

What should I do, Leslie?

I'm tempted. Oh, so tempted. But I feel as if I'm about to slide down a hill—if I take one more step, I'll lose control.

Oh, God.

Karen

Dear Karen,

But John's invitation is heaven-sent! Don't you think so? Yesterday you said you had no clue where to spend your holidays. You said you hated the thought of saying good-bye to both of them. And now you even know he can kiss! (Grin!) So what's stopping you? What's the problem? Go, grab a few days of fun, then turn around and go home. It's easy. Forget your scruples. And hold on to your heart.

Leslie

Dear Leslie,

Thank you for your lightning-fast reply. Yes, yes, of course you're right. It's no big deal.

I know.

I know.

But still . . . I couldn't think about anything else all evening, and I fed the little woodstove three times more wood than it can stomach, until it all but exploded.

I churned it over and over in my mind.

What if I bite off more than I can chew?

God, I'm such a chicken. But I would hate to hurt John. Hate to hurt me too.

What shall I do???

Karen

Dear Karen,

Of course that trip and all it entails might mean you will get close, closer than you might want right now. But if you step back from the challenge, how will you ever know if it could have worked out? Didn't you write a few days ago that life is all about decisions? Go for it.

Leslie

Dear Leslie,

I'm hurting all over. Had to take them to Jackson Hole airport tonight and send them off. It turned out to be mighty complicated with Gerry's crutches and his luggage, and I did open my eyes wide at the tickets for the first-class seats they had booked to allow Gerry to put up his foot during the flight. But I think the insurance will cover part of it.

Just before they had to go through the security check, Gerry said, "So, will you come to see us, Karen?"

"I'll think about it."

His face fell. "But why don't you want to come? Seattle is fantastic."

"Yes. Yes, I don't doubt it." In my mind, I batted away the image of a mud-covered tent. "I just have to sort out some other things, but I'll tell you on the phone about my decision, okay?"

"Okay." He turned away, his shoulders drooping.

John tilted up my chin and said, "I would love for you to come, Karen. And you needn't be afraid, you know. There are no strings attached."

And with that, his lips brushed mine, and then he was gone.

I was left standing on my own, eyes smarting, feeling like a complete idiot.

A lonely idiot too.

Karen

Dear Idiot,
You know how to make yourself happy again. It's in your hands.

Love,
Leslie

Dear Leslie,

I've thought about it some more. I'll go.

I feel jumpy about it, much like a scared chicken venturing out into the world, and I hope nobody will say "Baa" to me on the plane, because then I'll jump right off again, with the state my nerves are in.

But I'll do it.

After all, what is life if you never risk anything?

Safe.

Do I want safety? Sort of. I'm a gypsy with a hankering for safety. Not very logical, but there it is. So keep your fingers crossed for me.

I had my final talk with Carl today. He was about as welcoming as an old lemon, but I got another contract for the next season! Hurray! I'm so relieved!

He also wished me happiness on my wedding, which I had completely forgotten. Then he asked where we would go on our honeymoon. Some little devil got into me, and I replied,

"The Antarctic. I've always had a hankering to visit some penguins."

And now I'm racking my brain to remember if penguins live in the Arctic or in the Antarctic, because I keep mixing up the two. Ahhh.

I've just booked my flight to Seattle, and I don't think I've ever been in such a state about anything at all.

Have a good rest tonight in spite of my disturbed e-mails,
Karen

Hi, Karen,

Hurray! I'm proud of you. Mistress of your scruples! You rock, girl!

But the Antarctic? What's sexy about seven layers of clothes?

Leslie

Dear Leslie,

I made a clean breast of it tonight: I told Candy and Terry that I will spend some time in Seattle in order to make up for our canceled cross-country tour.

Candy got to the point like lightning. "You're going to see John," she said.

I admitted I was.

"And where will you stay?"

"At his house. Where else?"

Her eyes grew wide. "But, Karen, you can't do that. You don't know him all that well."

"And why shouldn't I go?" I said, nettled. I didn't want to admit I had felt pretty much the same, but her next words revealed she was afraid of quite different things:

"What if he turns out to be someone you can't trust? Someone who's dangerous?"

"I can always leave and look for a hotel."

"Ah," she said darkly, "but it may be too late."

I stared at her. "You mean he might be a mass murderer?"

"Well, you never know."

The thought that something heinous could hide behind those gray eyes had never crossed my mind, and I'm afraid I started to laugh.

Candy gave Terry a little push. "Go on, you say something. Maybe she'll listen to you. It's not safe to roam about the country, visiting men she hardly knows." She made it sound as if it was a bad habit of mine.

I braced myself for more opposition, but Terry shook his head, not a feather ruffled, and said, "You leave her alone, Candy. She'll be fine with John."

I was speechless.

But when I re-found my voice and pressed him for details, asking how on earth he could be sure about it, he only shrugged and said, "It stands to reason."

Whatever that might mean.

And you can stop shaking your head now. Not everybody moves about the world as confidently as you do, my dear. We all have our little fears to bind and gag at regular intervals, and it beats me how the little critters always manage to escape again.

Have bought an extra bag of M&M's to be prepared for every crisis, but I think with the state my nerves are in, I'll have finished them before I reach the airport.

Karen

Dear Karen,

I can't believe Candy said that! Just when you had overcome your scruples and dared to get a life. Now, don't you listen to her. Terry is right. You'll be fine. Have a good flight, and keep me updated!

Leslie

Dear Leslie,

My flight to Seattle will leave in a quarter of an hour.

I AM SO NERVOUS.

I have to go to the bathroom every five minutes! I pity my neighbors if it should continue on the plane. And me.

I'm cold.

No, hot.

I think cold.

Oh, my God.

I have to switch off my laptop now.

THINK OF ME!

Karen

Chapter Five

Seattle

Dear Leslie,

It's all over.

I'm at the airport in Seattle, waiting for my flight back. I feel so stupid and small, you can't believe it. I'll write it all down for you; maybe it'll help me become less muddled.

At first it was wonderful. I saw the guys immediately when I came through the exit at the airport yesterday. They held a banner between them, saying *Welcome, Karen!* in crooked letters on what looked suspiciously like an old towel.

A huge wave of happiness engulfed me and made me choke. They took me to some sort of superJeep, and off we went. The night was overcast, and I didn't see much; I just enjoyed being close to them again. I believe we were a little crazy. We all talked at the same time; Gerry kept pointing out things to me that flashed by much too quickly to see, and John told me about Gerry's leg, and I told them about my flight. . . . I loved being with them, and I loved having that odd feeling of coming home, though it didn't make sense at all, of course.

I had been right to come, I thought. All would be well.

They finally swept me into a large building, situated in a kind of park, and I thought it must be a row of condominiums in a lovely setting, and then we ended up in a big, comfy kitchen with cozy lights. It was too late to eat; besides, I wasn't hungry, but we had a drink, and then my face kept splitting in two with huge yawns because of all the tension falling off my shoulders—my sleepless nights caught up with me.

"I think Karen needs to go to bed," John said with a grin.

"Dad! She only just arrived!"

"Well, look at her. Does she look as if she'll stay awake another hour?"

Gerry scrutinized my face and said, "I thought you were a night owl, Karen. Didn't you say so?"

I yawned. "Unfortunately, your dad is right. A bed sounds very tempting."

So they showed me to my room, which I didn't take in at all, having slipped into a semi-comatose condition in the meantime. I dropped into bed, and my cheek had hardly touched the soft pillow when I was already asleep.

The next morning a lark sang next to my window. I didn't know at first where I was and why I was so happy, but finally it all came back to me. The sun peeked through a set of long curtains made of deep red brocade. The muted rays filled the whole room with a magic light.

With the exception of that delirious birdsong, I didn't hear a thing, as if I was all alone in the whole house, and it sat breathing silently, waiting for me to wake up.

I sat up, wondering whose room this usually was. Not Gerry's—that much was sure. No saxophone paraphernalia anywhere, no posters.

Not John's either. It seemed a feminine room, somehow, though I couldn't tell you why. I didn't see any female stuff around. It was just so much in harmony. On the floor, my bare feet touched honey-colored wooden boards, covered in parts by a thick, creamy carpet that keeps you busy a whole lifetime if you want it to be clean. It didn't have a spot, though.

I ambled over to the bathroom with the happy feeling of being on a wonderful vacation. It was past eleven already, but what can you expect from a sleeper like me? I suspect the uneasy nights before had caught up with me.

When I opened the door to the bathroom, I saw with a shock that it was larger than my entire room at the guesthouse. I had not noticed yesterday, still groggy from the flight. I tiptoed in and peered about, sniffing out the corners like a dog checking new territory.

And that was when my day started to go downhill.

Now, don't get me wrong. It was lovely, designed with taste and love for detail. The tub was a whirlpool. The tiles beneath my feet warmed my toes, due to some hidden radiator underneath. On a gleaming railing I discovered a towel that could cover me from head to toe, not once but twice. It was so fluffy, my hands didn't want to let go again. Its fresh fragrance wafted up to me. Lavender, I think.

I stared around, feeling out of place like a street mongrel that had just trailed in, smelling of garbage. Had they booked me into some sort of luxury hotel?

It was odd.

Anyway, I took a shower and dressed in the most elegant stuff I could find in my suitcase (but it didn't get any better than jeans and a sweater) and ventured out into the hallway. In front of my door I found a letter. I picked it up.

Hope you slept well and long. We didn't have the heart to wake you up on your first day. Gerry had to go to school, and I'm at work, but call me when you're ready, and I'll come over immediately. In the meantime, Tabby will help you find everything you need. She'll be in the kitchen. John.

So. I turned right to get to the stairs that would lead me to the kitchen. But somehow I missed them.

I wandered on and on, until I came to some grand gallery around an entrance hall. I couldn't remember seeing it yesterday. It looked like a picture you'd see in those glossy magazines. Lord-of-the-manor stuff. I felt like a trespasser but figured if I stepped downstairs here and turned back in the direction I had come, I would sooner or later end up in the kitchen.

I didn't.

I lost myself in the maze of rooms and hallways, like Alice in Wonderland. And there was nobody, nobody at all. I tiptoed around like an intruder and wondered when the security alarm would start so the police could throw me out.

I was thoroughly rattled by the time I finally collapsed into a big leather armchair in a library that seemed to be one of the few places where people actually lived. At least the chair had some marks on the armrests, and a tiny piece of coal sat in front of the open fireplace.

The door opened, and a woman with a sour expression on her walnut face poked her nose in. "Are you Karen?" she said in a voice that made me think of the witch in "Hansel and Gretel."

I shook myself. "That's me!" I replied with artful cheerfulness.

The witch gave me the once-over, her mouth working silently. "I'm Tabby. Will you come to the kitchen, please?"

I jumped up. Maybe I had desecrated some sanctuary.

Darn John. Why did he drop me in this palace and leave me all alone with a disapproving woman?

I followed her, crushed by my surroundings. The kitchen wasn't far, but I still wouldn't have found it without her help. I hate this place!

Tabby made me sit at the big scrubbed table that had seemed so friendly yesterday.

"Coffee or tea?" she asked.

"Er. Coffee, please."

"Bacon and eggs?"

"No, thanks."

"A soft-boiled egg, then?"

I stared at her. It felt like unfriendly hotel service. Never in my whole life had I imagined it would turn out like this. I had imagined John, Gerry, and I getting breakfast together, laughing and chatting and planning the day. The disappointment made my eyes sting.

I said I would like a soft egg, but I would do it myself. Big mistake. Tabby told me in no uncertain terms she would not let me boil an egg in her kitchen. Okay, she wasn't as rude as that, but the message was clear. I felt so lonely and out of place, Leslie, and it got worse by the minute. Next, Tabby asked me why I hadn't come to the kitchen, as I had been told to. Guess how clever I felt when I had to admit I hadn't found the way!

But worse was to come. I figured that since I was sitting there, condemned to do nothing, I might just as well find out more about this place. "Is this a sort of condominium?" I asked.

"What?" She stared at me.

I made a move with my hand. "This place. It's huge. Who lives here?"

"John, Gerry, and I do," she replied with a withering glance that seemed to say, "And where did you grow up? In a chicken coop?"

I swallowed, not believing it. "But . . . but it's immense." I squeezed out. "How many bedrooms are there?"

"Twelve."

"Twelve?" I gasped. "How can three people need twelve bedrooms?"

I got another glance that should have frozen the blood in my veins. "Are you a communist?"

"No! No, I'm just a normal middle-class citizen, and I thought John was too! I had no clue he lived in a palace!"

It was her turn to stare. "But don't you know?"

I jumped up, my nerves fraying at the ends like chewed-on strings. "What? What do I have to know?"

"He's the owner and CEO of ON!"

I dropped back into my seat as if electrocuted.

Sure, John had talked about electronics with me. He told me he had built up a company and that he loved his job.

Right.

But had he told me he had happened to build up the largest American company for electronic equipment? Had he told me he was the owner of ON!, for God's sake, which has several thousand employees, as everybody knows, even people like me, who know NOTHING about the world of electronics? I should have Googled him long ago, but it just never crossed my mind.

If he had been in the kitchen at that moment, I would have strangled him without any further ado. How dare he mislead me? How DARE he?

"So," I said in a barely controlled voice, "this is his house?"

"Sure." She probably thought I was straight from a slum. "Has been for almost five years."

"I see." I had to get out of there. But I couldn't very well bolt, not with her wrinkled face watching me. So I squeezed down my perfect egg and gulped up the fresh first-class coffee, then pushed back my chair and said, "Thank you. I'd like to go to town in a little while. How do I call a cab?"

"John said you could take the Benz if you wanted to go out."

Right. The Benz. What next?

I swallowed and said, "That's great, but as I don't know my way around, I think I'd prefer a cab."

"But didn't John want to come and join you?"

"Er. No. Not yet."

"You can take the Benz anyway." She took a key from a row of hooks next to the door and held it out to me. "It's equipped with a navigation system."

I was stuck. At least she didn't mention a chauffeur.

Inwardly fuming, I took the keys, nodded, and stalked off. I didn't dare call a taxi now, afraid that Tabby would immediately contact John and tell him I had refused to drive his precious Benz.

I managed to find my room by taking the same stairs as yesterday. They are a kind of backstage stairs (though you wouldn't notice by looking at them), and the entrance on the hallway upstairs is closed off by a door that looks like a normal door to a room. No wonder I hadn't found it!

I threw the few things I had unpacked into my suitcase, ran downstairs again, managed to locate the garage that housed the Benz (besides a few other precious machines), parked it right in front of the side door we'd used yesterday evening to get into the house, and—making sure Tabby was busy in the kitchen—smuggled my suitcase and myself out of the house.

I was already starting the engine when I realized I should leave some kind of message for John. So I ran upstairs to my room once more, found a box with embossed (!) stationery in a drawer, and sat for some time, chewing on the fountain pen (made of solid gold, or so I think). Finally, I wrote,

Dear John, I'm sorry, but our worlds just don't match. All the best, Karen.

I know, I know, it's not the world's best letter, and you would have done better, but I just couldn't find any other words.

I only breathed freely when I had left the property. As soon as it was out of sight (and that took a while, I tell you!), I parked at the curb and fought for about twenty minutes with the navigation system in order to convince it to reveal the way to the airport. How was I to know it's called SeaTac and that you have to address an airport by name in order to find it!

But I managed.

I stuck the parking ticket behind the windshield wiper, wondering if someone would steal it. Well, if they do, I figure John can afford the fine. I'll send him a text with the exact parking location as soon as I'm at a safe distance. After all, it won't be as if he'll miss it—he has enough cars to tide him over.

So here I am now, sitting on one of those lovely plastic seats at the airport, waiting for my flight to be called. Unfortunately, I have to wait two hours, but if John works his usual hours, he won't notice the time and won't wonder about my not calling.

I hope.

I have switched off my cell phone, so he can't reach me. I can't talk to him.

I'm not sure if you understand, Leslie.

It may sound as if I overreacted. I know there are loads of women who would count themselves lucky in my situation. But you, you know me so well, you will understand, won't you?

It's just that . . . all that money, it . . . it will swallow me. I'll lose myself, lose my identity in that place.

And how can a ski teacher and partial bookshop owner be on a par in a relationship with a tycoon? It would never work.

I would always be in a weaker position, would always hang on by an inch, would always feel out of place.

I had worked myself up to forgo some of my independence. You know how I hate that thought. I was even ready to start a relationship, and taking the plane to Seattle was a momentous decision for me, knowing what it might entail.

But now, it's all over. I can't imagine we could ever be on the same level. I do so hope you understand, though it's a bit complicated.

And why, why, why did he never let on? I can't imagine how stupid I was. I feel so humiliated.

Leslie, I just glanced up, and there's a man at the counter. His back looks a lot like John's.

It can't be, though. John is still at work.

He just turned around.

It IS John.

He looks ready to kill me.

Oh, God.

Karen, switch on your darn phone and CALL ME!
Stay right where you are. Don't run away from John!
                                        Leslie

Dear Leslie,

I'm sorry I left you hanging. Your message on my cell sounded freaked out, and I know it took me ages to reply to your e-mail, but it all happened like an avalanche. . . . So here's what happened:

John strode up to my plastic seat while I cowered behind my laptop, doing my best to become invisible.

He ground to a stop in front of me, and I have to say, I didn't feel good. His anthracite suit and white shirt made him look formidable, but the worst was the expression in his eyes. They snapped with wrath and something else, but I didn't have the time to figure it out because I was still concentrating on becoming invisible.

"What on earth do you think you're doing, running away like this?" His voice was low but compressed by fury.

"I'm not 'running away'!" I wished my voiced didn't shake so much.

"Oh, no? Well, it surely looks like it to me! Couldn't you wait for me to return? Couldn't you call me and explain? I thought we were friends! Is this what you do to your friends?"

I pushed my laptop aside and jumped up, fists on my hips. "You're a fine one to talk! Is it par for the course to deceive your friends? To pretend to be someone you aren't? To lie all the time?"

He grabbed me by the shoulders. "I didn't lie to you!"

"Oh, no," I spat. "Of course not! You told me you were a gazillionaire with a twelve-bedroom house and a multibillion-dollar company, didn't you? Just when did you do that? I must have overheard it!"

"Why should I?" His eyes were like quartz. "Why should it make any darn difference if I'm wealthy?"

"Because . . ." I tried to swallow, but I couldn't, my throat hurt so much. "Because it defines you! It's your environment, your world; it defines the things you take for granted, the things you see and deal with, the stuff that impresses itself upon you!" Do you understand what I wish to say, Leslie? He didn't.

His hands dropped from my shoulders as if I had hit him. "And is that all I am? What my 'environment' made of me? Thank you very much, Karen!"

And suddenly I understood that other expression in his eyes. He was hurt. My fury evaporated into nothing, leaving me stupid and raw, but he was already continuing.

"I thought we had something going between us, Karen. An understanding. Something so precious to me, I wanted to do anything to be close to you. But apparently it's not the same with you."

I stared into his eyes, frozen by his words. Finally I found my voice. "It is! It was! I would never have come if I hadn't felt the same!"

"So what makes you run away at the slightest hitch, searching for cover, leaving me a darn NOTE saying our worlds don't match?"

I'm afraid I burst into tears. You know I barely ever cry. I think it scared me more than him.

Sniveling, I finally mumbled, "But they don't match, John."

"Because I'm rich and you're not? What kind of a stupid reason is that?" His voice had softened.

Suddenly I was exhausted. I dropped back onto the plastic seat and covered my face with my hands. When something creaked beside me, I turned my head. John had lowered himself into the seat next to me and was watching me with an expression that made my insides feel like jelly.

"There's something else to it, isn't there?" he asked softly.

I shrugged. "I don't know. Yes. No. I don't know."

For some reason, he seemed to be able to make sense out of me.

"Tell me."

I stared at my hands, gulped, and told him all about my father, who left us when I was four, how long it took my mother to get out of the financial and emotional mud, and that she had imprinted one truth in my mind, again and again. Don't ever become dependent on someone else. She even made me promise I would stick to that when she died. Those were her last words. Have I ever told you that, Leslie? I think I haven't; I tried to forget it for so long. It's my heritage, if you want.

He was quiet for a time, digesting my words.

Then he said, "But you said you've got a partner in your bookstore. That's a dependency."

Trust him to put his finger on the spot. "Yes. I couldn't sleep for a week before I signed the contract." (I think that's another thing I never told you, Leslie.)

"And have you regretted it?"

"Um. No."

"So maybe, maybe, your mother wasn't always right?"

"Hmm."

His gray eyes bored into me, and I had to swallow, but I stuck to my guns. "John, why didn't you tell me?"

It was his turn to look uncomfortable. "It was Gerry's idea."

"Gerry's?" I couldn't believe it, but then John explained how Gerry had had to change schools when he moved in with John, and that one kid in the new school thought it entertaining to tease him about being a gazillionaire's son. A softy. Someone who couldn't manage anything on his own if it weren't for his father.

I flinched, but John continued, "When we had that day at Christmas, the one I told you about, it all burst out of him. He said he would like the world to see him just as himself and not as a rich man's son."

I closed my eyes. Oh, God. Trust me to put my foot in it.

"That's why we booked a 'normal' skiing tour. That's why we stayed at your guesthouse and not at some five-star luxury resort. For Gerry, it was an adventure. He loved every minute of it."

"And you?"

He looked at me for a long time. "I did too."

Then he asked me what had happened in the morning to make me run. He said Tabby had called him, telling him I had gone to town, and that I had left a message.

I was furious when I heard that. "I left the letter in my room! She was not supposed to find it!"

"She probably went up to make your bed."

Can you imagine that, Leslie? To have your bed made by someone else? I never even thought of that. It seems Tabby is John's housekeeper. I told him she hates me, but he believes she's afraid I'll kick her out.

When he said that, I couldn't believe my ears. "Say that again?"

He grinned. "She thinks two women in the same house won't work."

"She can relax. I'll never move into that house."

John swallowed. "I see."

I wasn't so sure if he did. "Would you move into my trailer?" I asked.

His jaw sagged.

I nodded, satisfied and sad at the same time. "Exactly. Your house is as alien to me as my trailer is to you. And that's what I mean when I say our worlds don't match. Whenever there's a choice, it will be your choice, the gazillionaire's choice. I'll be a little appendix, something tagged on for decoration only. My world will be swallowed up by yours. I'll lose myself."

Something dawned in his eyes, something that gave me the feeling he might understand after all, contorted as it was. Can you understand me, Leslie? I think you do, but then, you've known me ever since we were teenagers, and you've had plenty of time to get used to my spleens.

I told John that my fear of losing myself was the reason I'd hesitated so long before coming.

"But you didn't know back then that I was in another world, as you phrase it."

"No. But what's easier to sell? A complete electronics company or the share in a tiny bookstore? What's easier to find? A new school for an already uprooted teenager or a new job for a skiing teacher?"

His eyebrows arched. "You're talking commitment here."

I pulled up short. Oh, God. I was. I was scared by my own thoughts. Where had they come from? What we had shared so far? Just one almost kiss, one thank-you kiss, and one passionate kiss . . . that was it. I realized I was going over the edge. I bit my lip, grabbed my laptop, and tried to get away, scuttling sideways like a crab.

He stopped me with one simple question. "So how many bedrooms could you accept at the max?"

At first I thought I had misunderstood him.

"We can work it out, you know," he said, with that devastating smile of his.

I groped around until I could remember my other headache. "You forget the little matter of passion," I said.

He blinked. "What passion?"

"You said it at the hospital. 'A little bit of passion' doesn't make sense. Don't you remember?"

"I do. But I have thought about it, and I think I've found a solution."

I laughed, looking at the laptop. It was a curious sound, bitter and without any mirth at all. "Forget it. If you are a passionate person, you can't just switch it off. Whatever you do, you do it one hundred percent. I should know. I am one."

"I know. It's one of the reasons I love you."

My head snapped up at that, and, Leslie, I can't describe the way he looked at me. With a kind of crooked grin that tore something in two right inside of me.

"I hadn't pictured it quite like this," John said, gesturing at the loud and noisy hall, the plastic seats, and the old blob of chewing gum next to his shoes, "but it seems I have to tell you now to make you stay."

I was struck dumb and could do nothing but stare at him.

"About the passion," he continued. "There are millions of other people who work with passion and love with passion at the same time. Why shouldn't we manage it too? I believe the answer is slices."

"Slices," I repeated, shaking my head, thinking I had finally lost it and didn't understand his language anymore.

"Yeah. You slice your life into segments, and within the slices, you can be as passionate as you please. The important thing is to keep the equilibrium among the slices."

"Like a pie?"

"Yes."

"Right." It sounded good. If somewhat theoretical. But then, he's a newcomer to this. So am I.

What do you think of slices, Leslie?

When I still hesitated, John told me we didn't have to make any momentous decisions right away. He said we could let it grow on us, and that many things sort themselves out without our help if we wait.

For an instant I heard your voice saying the very same thing. But there's a point of no return in everything. Or at least a point where you can't return without leaving a limb behind.

Say, a leg or an arm. Nothing essential, but still. At that point I saw you throwing back your head, laughing, saying I'm a chicken. The worst chickenhearted chicken you've ever met.

So I pulled myself together, zipped up the bag of my laptop, and, feeling as if I was setting fire to all bridges behind me, I said, "Is there a place in Seattle where they sell M&M's? I sorely need a big bag."

John grinned. "We'll find one."

And then he bent forward and kissed me, and it felt so tender and glad, I sort of melted and wondered how I could ever have been so confused.

After a trip to the supermarket, we went home, and he fixed us an omelet. It tasted great, but he said that was the whole range of cuisine he could manage. No wonder, if he's always had a housekeeper.

I think he was afraid to let me out of sight lest I do another vanishing act, and since his house makes me feel like a cat on a hot tin roof, he schlepped me to Discovery Park.

Discovery Park, as I have learned today, is the largest nature park in Seattle and makes you feel you're in the middle of the wilderness, though, in fact, it's somewhere in the center of the city. There's a lighthouse too—and a breathtaking view across Puget Sound. Maybe John thought being there would make me feel more at home. Sound thinking. I liked it.

We returned windblown and tired. Soon afterward Gerry came home, and John took us out to a small Persian restaurant: Pomegranate and plum sauce with dark, spicy meat, accompanied by fragrant rice and sweet mint tea. John seems to have discovered my love for unusual food.

Gerry, blissfully unaware of the drama he had missed, chatted about a million things, while John contented himself with smiling at me in a way that pushed my level of adrenaline to unforeseen heights.

My mind was in a turmoil when I finally returned to my

glamorous room, but I thought it would help if I wrote it all down, and that's why you are on the receiving end of this ten-mile-long e-mail. Did I tell you I'm sitting right now with crossed legs on my luxurious bedspread that is so soft, it feels like being nestled into a cloud? The interior designer who did it sure knew her stuff.

The luxury and sheer space of the house still feel scary, but at least I know now that John's and Gerry's rooms are right next to mine. It seems they center their activities in this farthest tip of the left wing of the house, leaving the rest for occasional use only, never noticing how odd this is. Humph.

I'll keep you informed about my progress into the world of the rich.

Karen

Dear Karen,

No, you never told me about that promise to your mother before she died. I can't believe she did that to you! I'm so glad you told John. It will make him understand much better why you freaked out. This concept of slices sounds a bit odd, but if it works for you both, go for it.

A book with "profound sayings" fell into my hands today. You know how I hate them—a pat saying for every catastrophe—but it opened at one page, and when I read it, I wondered if I should start to believe in fate after all. It said, "Fear cripples" (and then it continued with some other mushy wisdom, but I promptly forgot it).

Don't allow yourself to be crippled.

Leslie

Dear Leslie,

Thank you for your advice. You're so right. I'm keeping my fear on tight reins, and I realize that I am relaxing bit by bit.

You won't believe who I met today. I woke up early this morning—well, before ten o'clock, that is. Found my way to the kitchen (hurray!) and made myself a cup of coffee. Thank God Tabby wasn't there. John had told me he would leave early (when he says that, he means he hits his office desk by six A.M.!) and asked me about four times if it was okay with me and that he would come and join me immediately after I had woken up. Feeling a tad more comfortable in his palace, I decided to wake up properly first and only call him afterward.

So I sat at the kitchen table, trying not to hit my teeth on the rim of the coffee mug, when a knock on the side door ripped through the morning.

I dragged myself up and opened it. A slim woman stood in front of me. She stared at me as if I was an apparition.

"Oh, hi," she finally said in a voice that sounded like caramel. "Could I talk to Tabby, please?"

"I'm sorry, I don't know if she's in," I said. "I just got up and haven't seen her yet."

Her eyes grew wide. Lovely eyes, by the way. Clear and blue. She leaned toward me, so her coppery hair slid forward over her shoulders. "Who are you?"

"I'm Karen." And as she only looked a question, I added, "I'm a friend of John and Gerry."

It seems John doesn't have any friends. Or at least none that stay overnight. (I'm not sure if that's good or bad.) Her mouth dropped open, and she stepped into the kitchen as if she belonged there.

"John's friend?" she asked, scrutinizing me from my feet in socks to my old sweater.

I couldn't help comparing my outfit to her suede leather moccasins, perfectly fitting chinos, and crisp linen blouse.

Suddenly she thrust out her hand and said, "I'm Celina, John's ex-wife."

Oh, God. Oh, God. Instantly I wished I had called John already, had gotten instructions on how to deal with ex-wives, had not gotten up at all!

I recoiled but managed to get a grip on myself, shake her hand, and invite her in for coffee, but she refused.

"I just wanted to drop off a sweatshirt Gerry has asked for," she said. "It's from a jazz summer camp, and when he moved to his father's, we couldn't find it. But he's very attached to it." She held up a glossy bag that looked as if it had housed a five-hundred-dollar scarf before it came here.

I stared at her. You know what, Leslie? She seemed nice. Really nice. I felt confused, as I had pictured her to be an icy blond.

"Oh," I finally managed to say, "Gerry will be delighted. What a shame you missed him." However, I kept wondering if she had wanted to miss him. After all, it's no surprise that he's at school at ten on a normal weekday, is it? Then she said something that floored me.

"John's at work, I take it?"

I would have loved to say, "No, he's taking a shower," but I couldn't. So I just nodded.

"He hasn't changed." She smiled again. "Hope you won't be bored. See you, Karen."

And with that, she gave a little wave of her hand, jumped into her silver convertible, and drove off in a terrifying cloud of exhaust.

And I rushed to my room to write you this latest development!
Karen

Dear Karen,
  You say the ex is NICE? Wake up, girl! That parting dig had enough venom for three cobras. Stay out of her way, if you can.

  Leslie

Chapter Six

Dear Leslie,

If you are a gazillionaire, trying to impress a woman in Seattle in April, you will find a thousand things to do to enchant the lady in question.

If you are a gazillionaire, trying to impress a certain woman in Seattle in April who would far prefer you to be a normal middle-class citizen, choices diminish rapidly.

If, on top of that, the weather is not playing into your hands but proving to be as rainy as the Seattle reputation has it, then you might end up breaking out in a sweat.

These were, more or less, John's words when he arrived a little later—without having been called by yours truly, I might add.

When he had finished his tale of woe, I grinned. "Maybe you should ask Gerry for advice."

John arched his eyebrows. "We'd end up at the movies, eating popcorn."

"Why not? It's been ages since I've done that."

"Okay, that's noted. Is there anything else you'd like to see?"

I told him I wanted to ride your favorite subway, Leslie, or maybe I should say "upway," the Monorail.

"The Monorail?" He behaved as if I had proposed boarding a rocket to buy a bikini on the moon.

"Yes, isn't that the elevated train in the air, somewhere downtown?"

"Er. If you want to call it that, yes. I've never used it."

"Leslie said it's great fun."

"Oh, Leslie has been to Seattle?"

Darn. I wished I hadn't slipped that one out. "Hmm. Yes. Fifteen years ago. We . . . actually, we were here together. It was awful."

"Oh. But if Leslie liked the Monorail . . . ?"

"Leslie liked a guy here and would have eaten bird droppings on toast without batting an eye. She was way over the moon about him." (Stop protesting; you know it's true!)

"I see."

"Otherwise, I have no clue what might be interesting. You see, I didn't have time to find out what Seattle has to offer. . . ."

His dimples appeared. "Ah, I forgot. You're used to planning your trips in excruciating detail."

If it hadn't been for the dimples, I would have thrown the top of my empty eggshell at him. As it was, I gathered my dignity around me like a cloak, crossed my arms in front of my chest, and said, "Ha. Okay, you plan our day. I will just lean back and let myself be amused."

"Dear God," he replied, and he admitted he had a meeting he couldn't postpone that afternoon but that he planned to spend the whole weekend with me.

Disappointment made me swallow.

John saw it of course and said, "I'm so sorry, Karen, but it's not yet the way I'd like it to be."

"No, I'm sorry," I quickly replied. "It's selfish to expect you to spend every waking minute with me."

"But that's what I want." His smile deepened. "Did you say only every *waking* minute?" He got up, and I was looking forward to being thoroughly kissed, when he stumbled over Celina's bag. "What's this? Have you been shopping?"

"No." I sipped a bit more coffee. "Celina dropped it off. She brought a sweatshirt for Gerry."

John sat down again in slow motion. "Celina? Celina was here this morning?"

"Yep."

He stared at me. "What did she say?"

"Nothing special. She only stayed a minute."

His eyes never left my face. "I can't imagine she took your presence in stride."

"Well," I muttered, "she managed better than I did."

"Tell me about it."

So I did. Including the final dig, because that was still eating at me.

He jumped up. "Come with me."

"What? Where?"

"I'll show you."

And he dragged me out of the house, put me into the Jeep, and drove me downtown.

I still remember how you raved about downtown Seattle. I always thought it was because you were madly in love with Greg or Matt or whatever his name was, but now that I see it myself—completely unbiased and untainted, of course—I have to concede, you have a point there.

A little one.

Okay, I'll admit it.

It's gorgeous.

I think it's because of the bay (forgot its name, but you will know), right next to those glittering skyscrapers. And in the background there are blue mountains with white caps, making me itch with wanderlust. It's so curious to see the sea and mountains in one setting. Makes me feel as if my two worlds are crammed together in a high-speed mixer.

After twenty minutes or so John stopped in a reserved parking space right in front of a huge tower made solely of glass and witchcraft. He nodded at the uniformed man next to the glass door, took a firm hold of my arm, and led me through.

Rushing through, I caught a glimpse of the discreet logo etched into the glass walls and knew where we were heading. "Why are you taking me to your office?" I whispered. I had to whisper because it was all so grand and awe-inspiring.

"I want to show you something." He led the way into an elevator lined with golden lights and mirrors. The mirrors showed me that my hair looked as if it was a temporary bird-home, but I couldn't do anything about it.

At the top floor, we got out. John took my hand and led me to an office with large windows and an even larger desk. An assistant looked up, surprise written large on her face. She had one of those perfect hairdos that don't even change in a gale.

"Sandra, I'd like to present Karen to you," John said. "Whenever she calls, put her right through, even if I have said I don't wish to be interrupted by anyone. Whenever she comes to this office, don't make her wait, no matter who is with me."

I didn't believe what I heard, and I think she felt stunned too. But she was well-trained—I have to hand her that. Getting up, she shook my hand, smiled, and said, "Of course, John. Nice to meet you, Karen."

I'm afraid I wasn't as well trained. My mouth went slack, and I stared at John as if he had lost his mind. He ushered me through into his personal office, but when he turned to close the door behind us, I glanced back at Sandra. Her eyes were out on stalks, and she gripped the chair next to her as if afraid of falling. It gave me hope that she was human after all.

John's office surprised me.

It has yellow walls!

No, I don't mean a sort of elegant buff beige; I mean yellow. Not screaming yellow either but a deep, sunny yellow.

I blinked, and John grinned. "It gets me through the winter," he said.

My gaze was drawn to the windows. The steep slope that defines downtown Seattle gives the skyscrapers a special effect, as you don't only stare at the wall of the building opposite you (the way you do in Manhattan), but you oversee everything below you, including the bay covered with little nutshells mounted with white sails. It's magic. I stared and stared while John busied himself at his desk, tapping at his keyboard, closing and opening drawers.

"You count the boats all day?" I finally asked.

"Yep." I could hear the smile in his voice. "It's soothing. Would you step over here?"

I unglued myself from the window and went to his side.

He had spread out several sheets across his desk. I had no clue what he was up to, but apparently he expected me to look at the stuff and make some intelligent noises, so I did.

The first one was an organizational chart of ON! It looked like a sort of fir tree. At the top was his name, and then it spread out into ever finer units. I found the words *marketing* and *controlling, R&D* and *customer care*. Well, I saw a lot more, but those are the ones I can remember. I looked up, wondering if he was trying to impress me. "So?"

He gave me another sheet. Same tree. But the top box was missing. Instead, the other boxes had shifted somewhat, and John's name appeared only in one inferior box: *R&D*. He explained that *R&D* stands for *Research and Development*. I couldn't believe the implication and asked him if he was kidding.

He leaned against his desk. "No. Remember what I said about the slices? I'm slicing down my job. That's what I did this morning. I made a list of all the things I do. When I finished, I picked what I like most. Then I listed the remaining tasks and distributed them among my staff."

He looked as excited as a schoolboy, but he also admitted that it wouldn't be easy. "I'll have to hold myself back from meddling once I've handed over the responsibility. But I'll have more time for the stuff I love. And for the people I love."

He looked at me with a smile that gave me a heady feeling, as if I could fly if I applied myself just a bit. I took a deep breath. "I'm impressed."

"Good. Mind you, it'll take some time. I have to work on it some more and give my staff the time to adapt and learn. But within the next four to six months it should be finished."

So. That's that.

I think sometime soon I have to start to have a little confidence in him; otherwise, I'll need an urgent session with a shrink.

Karen

Dear Karen,

. . . my thoughts exactly! Enjoy the good feeling, and don't worry about the future. It will all work out fine.

Leslie

Dear Leslie,

Guess what I did this afternoon? I took the Benz (did I drop this casually enough?) to the Bellevue Square Shopping Emporium. Maybe I should say it the other way around—the Cadillac took me there, as I followed its directions blindly.

I got myself a new haircut (shorter and a few highlights) and some clothes that make me feel a bit more adequate to the surroundings. Among them was a deep red shirt with a scooped neckline that I put on immediately. And—hold your breath—a blouse! Haven't worn one all winter! With tiny buttons formed like spheres. No, no, I don't look like my grandmother in it; it's a sporty cut (I plan to wear it loose, with jeans). The color is a sort of turquoise that matches my eyes. At least I thought so in the shop. Am not so sure anymore, now that I see it in daylight.

Have to admit, I got a bit crazy at Victoria's Secret too and spent far more than is sensible.

But I had fun! It would have been better with you, though.

Tonight Gerry's band is doing a concert at his school. He's all excited about it—has been for weeks, in fact. I hope it won't be as horrible as the school concerts where I performed my miserable pieces on the guitar.

Karen

P.S. I just read an article about a company that makes wonderful sun awnings. How about a red-and-white-striped one for our store? It would look so summery and fun! We could give the kids matching candy and paint the outdoor displays red and white too. I think the buff yellow awning we have right now looks too weak, besides being dirty. What do you say?

Dear Karen,

A red-and-white-striped awning? I just can't picture it. I like the buff yellow, and I can't stand any more work being done around me. Even the sight of a hammer makes me twitch.

So, what did John say about the new outfit and hair and all?

Leslie

Dear Leslie,

When John came home from work, he dropped his attaché case onto a kitchen chair and loosened his tie with a sigh before leafing through the letters Tabby had placed on top of the microwave. It seems that's where they belong.

Gerry sat at the table too, polishing off a huge bowl of corn-flakes as if he had never heard the words *stage fright*.

I watched John, my chin in my hands, a bit disappointed that he should not have noticed my new outfit. After all, even Gerry asked if I had washed my hair (!) and why I looked "kind of different."

All at once John said, his gaze still on a phone bill or some other equally riveting document, "This looks fantastic."

Gerry raised his head in surprise. "What does?"

John finally glanced up and smiled into my eyes. "Karen does."

And so we left for the concert, me still high from the compliment, Gerry high with adrenaline, and John with his hand on my knee all during the drive.

Did I say in my last e-mail that I expected a horrible school concert? Well, it started the way it usually does: The auditorium smelled of dust and chewing gum, and I immediately felt like a student again. Though having John by my side made me wonder if maybe I should prepare myself for another stage in my life.

The lights went out.

A spotlight came on, highlighting a drummer in a corner of the empty stage. He started with a drumroll that made a shiver run down my back and quieted even the most gossipy mother.

Then, out of nowhere, came the sound of a flute, pure and clean. Everybody whipped around and stared. Finally we discovered the flute player: A tall girl with a ponytail marched down the center aisle like the Pied Piper.

Next came a trumpet from the gallery. It sounded so triumphant, it seemed to announce the arrival of a king. And then the musicians came from out of every corner, playing every instrument singly, then joining the others onstage. It was dramatic, and I suddenly found I was gripping John's hand without meaning to. They continued with the tune, the sound growing louder all the time, until the orchestra seemed complete, but I still couldn't make out Gerry. All at once a spotlight came on at the side, illuminating a saxophonist all dressed in black. Gerry. He was so familiar and yet so strange. I know he had worried about his leg, and that's why they gave him a sort of barstool to sit on. That was the last coherent thought I remember, because at that instant his music gripped me, blotting out every other sense.

He had panache, a conviction that threw me. As if he knew his place in the world and was happy in it. You know that, in general, school bands make me itch. But Gerry was so passionate, so excellent, that the spark flew across the auditorium until everybody tapped with the rhythm.

I had a lump in my throat, and I glanced at John, who stared at the stage as if he had never seen his son before. I whispered into his ear, "A little bit of passion, eh? I don't think so."

John gripped my hand harder and didn't move, transfixed by the sounds Gerry teased out of the instrument.

The concert ended with dance tunes, and one by one the band members came back into the audience and spread out among us until you thought the sound was everywhere, and then Gerry started another crazy piece from his place in the spotlight that simply blasted us out of our seats, and suddenly we found ourselves dancing in the aisles. Can you believe it?

I think I danced with the great-grandfather of a student (or so he looked) and John and a French teacher with crooked glasses and an exchange student (Italian?) and who knows who else? By the time the concert was over, we were all out of breath and laughing and shaking our heads in disbelief. It felt like a party!

And then the school principal, a thin guy with no hair at all but surprising magnetism, came to the microphone and said he hoped we'd enjoyed the night, and he would like to announce the winner of this year's John Philip Sousa Award: Gerry Bernett!

Pandemonium broke out. A million people came to congratulate John, and he looked as dazed as I felt, and then

Gerry came, hot and triumphant, and I was SO glad and felt so much a part of them, I accepted the congratulations that came my way as if they were my due. (Just in case you don't know—I didn't—the award is given every year to the best player of the school band.)

But the night wasn't over, and I have to say, the last bit really floored me. Because suddenly the principal stood in front of us and congratulated John. It seems he's one of the guys who believes Gerry's talent to be outstanding. In turn, Gerry is convinced the man is a cross between Louis Armstrong and Jesus, miracles dropping right and left whenever he moves.

I thought he looked familiar and racked my brains where I could have seen him before or who he reminded me of. Then he stretched out his hand, and as our eyes met, he frowned and said, "But I know you."

"You seem familiar too," I replied. "Did you ever spend a holiday on Long Island or go skiing in Wyoming?"

John looked from one to the other of us and grinned. "So you do know people in Seattle, after all, Karen."

The principal stared at me. "Karen. Karen?" His eyes widened. "Now I've got it! We were at summer camp together, in the Cascade Mountains. Some ten—no, fifteen—years ago."

My memory clicked. "You're Matt!"

"Yeah, I'm Brad Housten."

Oops. I was lucky the noise in the auditorium deafened him to the slight misnomer. I had just opened my mouth to say something revolutionary like, "Isn't the world a small place?" when he asked, "So, are you still in touch with Leslie?"

I was speechless. It seems you left a lasting impression, my dear. I tried to interest him in my life, but I wasn't deceived. The only time he listened was when I mentioned you. He asked for your address, and though I'm pretty sure you'll jump at the chance to get back in touch, I told him I would give you his e-mail, so you can take it from there. It's brad.housten@mercerhighschool.com, so have fun. But don't forget to write me every now and then in between.

Karen

P.S. Can you believe that Celina didn't come to the concert? It seems she had to prepare a big dinner for some important guests of her new husband. But I believe she hates the music-career idea so much, she refuses to see Gerry in concert. I know Gerry missed her—his gaze searched the auditorium the whole time. I hurt all over when I saw it and think I'll have to murder her. Make sure you've got the number of that defense attorney at hand.

P.P.S. Need I say it turned into a late night and that Gerry was so high, he went to bed long after we did, in our separate rooms?

Dear Karen,

You met BRAD HOUSTEN? I can't believe it! I'll send him an e-mail right away, to make him feel guilty that he stopped writing all those years ago. How nice to know I left a lasting impression somewhere. Maybe I can start a hot little flirtation. I've never flirted with a school principal in my life. It'll be a new experience!

Leslie

Dear Leslie,

Gerry, being now surrounded by music appreciation for the first time in his life, has decided he loves his new high school. That's what he revealed this morning, during our lazy Saturday-morning breakfast. Phew. No more talk of changing schools. Instead, we are discussing additional music courses and summer camps, and I believe that's a good compromise. John is relieved too.

I went up to brush my teeth before we left for our Monorail/sightseeing trip downtown, and while I did so,

Gerry ambled in, perched on the edge of the bathtub, and rehashed every minute of the concert. I was touched.

His father wouldn't saunter in here, uninhibited, as if I'd been part of the family forever. And while I got ready, we chatted on and on, and one thing led to another, and suddenly I heard myself asking him if he didn't want to invite his friends from the band for a prolonged fun session one weekend (after all, the twelve bedrooms have to be put to some use). Guess what. He loved the idea.

But as soon as the deed was done, I realized I hadn't run the idea by John. Who might hate it and veto the whole thing. What right did I have anyway to invite a whole BAND, for God's sake?

So I swallowed and trudged downstairs to 'fess up. I found John in the kitchen, which still smelled of toast and butter. He held a jar of strawberry jam in his hand.

"John?"

He glanced over his shoulder and smiled at me in the way he has that does things to my temperature. I quickly said, "I've just done something you might hate."

He raised his eyebrows. "You've booked an earlier return flight?"

"No. Oh, no."

"Then it can't be that bad."

"Well. I . . . I asked Gerry if he didn't want to invite the band here for a weekend."

"The . . . the band?" he asked in a failing voice, placing the jam on the table with care.

"Yup. The band."

"How many kids are in that band?"

"Uh. I'm . . . I'm not sure."

He dropped into a chair, bent his head forward until it was hidden in his hands, and started shaking.

I've never felt so bad in my life, Leslie.

Starting forward, I babbled, "Gosh, I'm sorry, John. I really don't want to push you into something you don't like. I'll ask Gerry to forget all about it. I should have discussed it with you first. But the idea kind of jumped out of my mouth and . . ."

He raised his head.

He was laughing!

A ton fell from my heart, and he caught my hands and pulled me close until I sat on his lap, and then he said, "It's quite okay if you invite a band to stay, Karen. Do you think we have to be here too? Or could we get away that particular weekend?"

The smell of his skin intoxicated me, but I managed to say, "I think we have to stay. Otherwise, they might take the house apart."

"Hmm. How unfortunate."

His dimples appeared, and he pulled me closer until his lips touched mine. His hands cupped my face, and the last thing I heard was the rain lashing against the windowpanes before I was reduced to his fingertips, and mine, and every inch of skin where we touched.

Gerry's door banged, and we jumped apart. Then Gerry galloped into the room. "Hi, Dad. Hi, Karen!"

John smiled at him. "I hear you're going to invite over half the school."

"Yeah. Cool, ain't it? I want to call Mr. Housten right away. Where's his number?" He started to rip off magnetic pins from the fridge and leafed through a telephone list.

John watched him. "Do you have to call Mr. Housten now? We're about to leave."

"Dad! It won't take long! I need to know what he thinks!"

I asked, "Why Mr. Housten?"

"He's the conductor of the band besides being the principal," John answered, but he was drowned out by a triumphant shout from Gerry, who clutched his list and stormed out the door again, presumably in search of a telephone.

Before the door had closed behind him, I was in John's arms again. It wasn't a conscious movement, more like automatic, as if we were magnets, drawn together no matter what. I wouldn't have minded a little bit of passion at that moment, but of course Gerry blustered down the stairs again before I could act on this admirable inclination. With a suppressed oath, John released me.

Gerry had an important message: Could we pack extra sandwiches? Breakfast had finished all of fifteen minutes ago, and he feared he would soon be in danger of starving.

"I've got a bag of M&M's," I proposed. (Yes, I know that doesn't surprise you.)

John laughed. "The true Karen Larsen Survival Kit."

When Gerry had left again like the jack-in-the-box he was, John crossed his arms in front of his chest and said, "I won't touch you again as long as Gerry is running around like this. It drives me nuts."

"What a shame."

He smiled at that. "By the way, will you inform Tabby about the impending takeover by a host of teenagers?"

I blanched. "God, I forgot that they'll need to be fed. Do we have to tell her?"

"Don't worry, I'll do it."

And I realized a bit late that he was teasing me. Then he forgot his rule and pulled me close again, and I went more than willingly, but of course Gerry soon exploded back into the room.

It seems Brad Housten is delighted with the idea of a whole weekend session. He proposed booking a special band teacher who's also a celebrity (Gerry gave us the name with shining eyes, but I've already forgotten it), so it will be a true event. Unfortunately, this means it won't take place until the end of May, by which time I will long since have returned to Long Island, leaving John to cope with it all alone. That earned me a sardonic glance from him. I'm a true friend.

Karen

Dear Karen,

You're incredible. First you don't want to stay and have a million scruples, and then you march right in and start to invite people into his home. That man loves you to bits if he puts up with that!

Did I tell you Brad answered right away? He said it was all due to some poor teenaged confusion that he stopped writing me. He's great fun, witty, and lighthearted, and now I have two reasons to check my e-mail every morning.

Leslie

Dear Leslie,

I'm delighted to hear you're having fun with Brad. You deserve it, after that catastrophe with Matthew last year.

The Monorail was great. Does this mean it's truly good, or does this mean I've reached a similar state as the one you were in when you saw it?

I mean, if you look at it in a sober kind of way, it's only an elevated subway.

Can't write more—we're about to leave for the movies.

Karen

P.S. John's arm hardly left my shoulders today. Funny how a little thing like that can make you so happy. Gerry saw it and grinned.

P.P.S. Candy sent me an e-mail tonight and asked if I was getting along well with the mass murderer. (It seems she typed it with one hand, and it took her about half an hour to finish one sentence.) I replied like lightning, telling her he had devoured me alive but that she needn't bother rescuing me.

Dear Karen,

Want an honest answer? It's not the Monorail. It's you. Or, rather, him.

Leslie

Dear Leslie,

I have to say that in spite of the aforementioned difficulties entertaining a certain woman, John does a good job.

A very good job indeed.

That's also why I haven't written for so long—sorry, m'dear.

Did you know there are about five million restaurants in Seattle? Well, no, that's not exactly a statistic from the town's Web site. It's a personal estimate from what I have seen. They're small, they're intimate, they have the most extraordinary food (Indonesian, Japanese, Polynesian—you name it, it's here), and they're all tucked away in little corners or behind skyscrapers where you would never suspect. I love them. Compared to that selection, Long Island offers fish. Full stop.

But my pleasures aren't all concerned with matters of the flesh: We even visited a museum called the Experience Music Project. Yes, Gerry's choice, of course. I found it a lot more interesting than expected, even with my nonexistent music genes. Felt weird to be there all together. Like a true family.

Yesterday the sun came out for more than five minutes on end, and I was surprised to see that Seattle can be blue. Really, really blue. I asked John if it happened more than a dozen times a year, and he gravely promised it. Am not sure if I can believe him.

But my resistance is crumbling. It may just be possible that Seattle is a town where you can live without contemplating quick ways for suicide within a fortnight.

Karen

Dear Karen,

Seattle is one of the most attractive towns in the States. Take it from me; I know. Brad agrees, by the way. He has turned into a much better correspondent than he was all those years ago.

With all your ravings, I can feel the need for a vacation

*coming on. Mrs. Bluebottle is giving me a hard time right
now, as if it's my fault that the next book from Annabel
Grandini hasn't come out yet.*

Leslie

Dear Leslie,

I'm sorry Mrs. Bluebottle is such a pain. If only she wasn't
one of our best customers! Also, I'm sorry I don't write more
often, but I have a bit of a feeling that someone else's e-mails
are making up for my omissions. For some unfathomable reason, clocks gather speed whenever John is around. He doesn't
mention any long-term commitment at all (clever man). Instead, he just shows me the best sides of Seattle, and I may
start to believe soon that it's a nice place.

He takes more time off work than I think is okay. After all,
he only returned from his skiing holiday a few weeks ago, but
whenever I ask about it, he brushes it aside. Today, it's Saturday, and he said he had a surprise for us and told us to dress in
our thickest fleece sweaters and rubber boots.

And guess where he took us?

On a whale-watching cruise! It was a blue (!) day again,
and as we boarded our vessel and found the sound stretched
out in front of us, I could already feel my spirits soaring.

I preferred not to ask John if he has his own yacht—I bet he
does. Instead (to avoid crushing the insecure female at his side),
he sensibly booked us on a tourist tour that cruises through
Saratoga Passage into the San Juan Islands. I'll show you the
pictures when I'm back, so I can point out every pebble that
fascinated me!

We were lucky; a whole group of Orcas was feeding. They're
awesome, Leslie. One ranged alongside the boat, its fin almost
touching us, and we could hear its breath hissing out. I think
their coloring makes them so impressive. The gray whale kind
of mingles with the sea in spite of its size, even more so if it has

that crust of shells on its back. But the Orcas are ink black and shiny, and if their pure white bottom side flashes out of the water, oh, my, then I do understand that a poor seal may get into a panic and do something foolish. I'm glad I'm not a seal.

A stiff breeze tore at our clothes, but I wasn't cold, and John and I remained standing on the upper deck for a long time. (Gerry preferred to go belowdecks and empty the snack bar—no surprise there.) I leaned with my back against John, held by his arms and feeling his chin resting on the top of my head. All around us we saw nothing but blue water, blue skies, and green islands, and I suddenly realized there were few moments in life closer to being perfect.

I try not to think of the day when I have to return. Crazy, ain't it?

First she doesn't want to go, then she doesn't want to leave. True female style.

Enjoy your flirtation with Brad!

Karen

P.S. Candy wrote today and said her wrist is getting better. It's still a bit stiff, though. She says she's getting so used to being served like a queen by Terry that she might pretend it's worse than it is.

P.P.S. Sure about the awning? I understand that you've suffered a lot of demolition and restructuring these last few months, but ours does look boring.

Dear Karen,

Please. No red and white awning this year. Maybe next, all right? Humor me.

You'll never guess what I bought today. I got a Seattle travel guide! Wonderful book.

I do understand that you'll have a hard time saying good-bye. But you can always go back, you know.

Leslie

Dear Leslie,

I'll return home tomorrow. And I've never felt so torn in my life. What I feared (or hoped?) did happen: A part of me is here and will remain here. A precious part, I should say.

I don't think I can go without making some promise, without leaving some kind of commitment. It feels so unfair to say to John, "Oh, thanks for a lovely time. See you later. Bye, honey."

But in spite of it all, I'm not yet ready for it.

I'm not ready to hand in my resignation at Teton Valley.

I'm even less ready to change anything in the other half of my life. I can't even bear to write it down.

I don't want to give up anything!

You know, I can't just blend John into my life. In order to be a couple, I would have to tear out my old life and start from scratch. But I don't want that. I want every single one of my different worlds. They're three now, and the juggling is becoming increasingly difficult.

You know, Leslie, it's one thing to spend an enchanted holiday together. And it's quite another to throw over what you've built up for years.

I can see you shaking your head, wondering if I will ever understand that I can only learn to swim by getting into the water.

I think I'll go to John now and try to explain. I hope he'll understand, though to him, it must feel like trying to understand what's going on inside a chicken's head.

Karen

Dear Karen,

Hey, girl, how often do I have to say it? Take it easy! You had a great vacation. That's fine. (By the way, I'm panting to get to Seattle too, now that even YOU admit

it's a great place.) Now you return to your work. That's
fine too. So what's the big deal? Relax!

Leslie

Dear Leslie,

Have I ever told you that he's . . .

I can't write it; it would sound too infatuated. John just took
my hands and said, "I know. Take your time, Karen. Why
don't you wait until the summer is over, and then take it from
there? As I said, there's no need to make any dramatic decisions right now."

I love him so.

Karen

. . . hey, I hope you love me too! After all, I said more
or less the same.

Leslie

Dear Leslie,

How could I forget to mention it? I love you too! Grin.

Karen

Chapter Seven

Long Island

Dear Leslie,

I can't tell you how strange it feels that you are in Seattle, and I'm at home. As if the world stands upside down.

If you had asked me six weeks ago, I would never have believed that you would be getting on like a house on fire with Brad—so much so that nothing holds you here as soon as I've settled back in and the store is revamped for spring.

But after all, why not?

I'm glad you like your B&B, and I do hope you'll also like John and Gerry when you go out together tonight. I'm nervous about you three meeting! It would be dreadful if you told me you have no clue why I find those two so fascinating.

I admit, I envy you. I miss John so much. And Gerry. And . . . everything.

Don't worry about our store. It's in top shape now (though you should have said yes to the new awning, you know!). I'm happy about the shelves, and the glued-in carpet-nooses look better than I thought.

I'll manage the May tourists. After all, it's just one week. You enjoy your vacation and the sightseeing!

Oh, by the way: Do you know where the key to the garage has gone? It's not on its hook anymore, and I've searched everywhere.

I just opened a credit note from Waters & Waters. They have only credited twenty books, not twenty-seven. They say we only returned twenty. Can you recall how many you packed?

The bell is ringing. Ha! Our first tourists are trooping in. Have to go and sell them new worlds to dream in.

Wish I was with you.

Karen

Dear Karen,

All right; I'll admit it. When you sent me your e-mail, the one where you bolted out of John's home, I found it a bit hard to understand your reaction, in spite of knowing you, your history, and your fierce streak of independence.

But yesterday, when John showed me through the twelve bedrooms et al, I suddenly felt overwhelmed and dwarfed. I apologize, my friend. The house is enough to make me feel totally inadequate, and now I can imagine what it did to you, with your inexplicable love for tiny spaces.

So I made sure I went outside to explore Seattle. It's FANTASTIC. Gerry and John are totally delightful, but I haven't seen Brad yet. He had to attend a special teachers' congress because someone else got ill. He'll only come back to Seattle tomorrow.

Tabby is great, though. I chatted an hour or so with her when we all had dinner in the kitchen. Can't imagine why you didn't hit it off.

Leslie

P.S. About the missing key: Did you check underneath the sink in the back? Sometimes the key falls off and slides beneath it.

Dear Leslie,

I'm so glad to hear you love Seattle and get along so well with John and Gerry. I was a little worried. After all, you never met before. I hope you'll like Brad when you meet him. It would be so awful if you didn't hit it off after all those e-mails.

John calls every day. Okay, okay, make that several times a day. We won't be able to keep this up for long, as we tend to interrupt each other's sleep. Stupid time difference!

I might end up being fast asleep, sprawled across the cash register one day. I hope when they'll find me, they'll try to tickle me before they call in the paramedics. Maybe I should put up an explanatory note on the bulletin board, just in case. Something along the lines of: *If you find the owner of this store in a lifeless condition, keep cool and wake her up by waving a few M&M's under her nose.*

I also have to interrupt our calls much too often, as our customers have developed a nasty habit of jumping up and down on my toes to get my attention.

John is not much into writing long e-mails. Is that a character flaw? Gerry is even worse.

I didn't think you could miss anybody so much. It's like a physical pain, making me cringe. Stupid things make my eyes water. Like the guy who happened to pay from a wallet that looks just like John's. It was made of black leather and somewhat deformed by the habit every man seems to have of keeping his wallet in his trouser pocket. So you see, quite unique.

Also, my heart beats faster and gives a queer little jump

every time I see John's number on the caller ID display. Do you think that could be counted as exercise? In the first weeks at the store I always feel like a toad, fat and squat, because I don't move as much as I do during the winter. My feet still hurt, though.

Karen

P.S. I can't believe you like Tabby and chatted for an hour with her! WHAT is your secret?

Have to go. More tourists are trooping in, asking for "light" books. Maybe we should put up a display that looks like a cloud. *Books to dream by—fluffy reads.* How about it?

Dear Karen,

Yeah, I had the same demand for "fluffy summer-reading books." We have to do something about that. I'll meet Brad today and am excited like a little schoolgirl. Can't write more—have to beautify myself!

Leslie

Dear Leslie,

I had forgotten how much my feet hurt in the beginning of the season from all the standing in the store!

After a long day, I schlepped myself to the jetty, dropped onto the boards, and dangled my sore feet in the water. Ahh. You can't imagine what bliss.

And as I sat there and stared across the blue, blue water twinkling at me in the sunlight, I suddenly felt as if my soul would fly off at any minute to soar above the waves, far, far away until I would meet the horizon and then somersault right into the blue sky. I'm so addicted to blue.

Blue skies, blue water. Blue mountains. As long as it's blue, I'm happy. A bubble of sheer happiness, pure and undiluted, rose inside me until I felt I would burst into song.

No, don't worry, it didn't happen. I remembered in time that we have a business to keep up and that singing on the jetty during sunset might lead to being viewed askance. Mrs. Bluebottle, for one, wouldn't approve. She would never understand how I can get high on blue (and nothing else). It's warmer here than in Seattle too. Feels almost summery.

We live in the most beautiful spot on the earth, don't we, Leslie? There's one drawback to skiing all winter. There are no smells (if you don't count wet wool, that is). I think that's why I always get into a kind of olfactory intoxication when I return to Long Island. That salty smell of the sea, the tang, the fragrance of wet earth and tar mingles together until I feel like a dog running around with my nose high in the wind to catch every nuance.

How I wish John was with me. How I miss the smell of his skin.

I sat there for ages, until I suddenly realized my feet had turned into frozen clumps and that I had better take them out pronto if I didn't want to end up with a cold, feeling blue in the head as well!

Karen

P.S. How was the meeting with Brad?

Dear blue friend,
    Enclosed, I send you a picture I'm sure you'll enjoy. I love every second here!

                                        Leslie

Dear Leslie,

The picture of you, John, and Gerry in front of the Space Needle is great. You look like a model family, you know. All happiness and fun.

Have to go. An entertaining kid just smeared his ice cream

all across the front window. Have to get onto my knees and start scrubbing. Gah.

Karen

Dear Leslie,

I guess you don't have much time to write right now, but I wanted to tell you that I found the key to the garage today. Guess where? In my high boots, the ones I'm so proud of, as I think they make me a little bit sexy. I put them underneath the sink to dry after that tropical rain last week. Well, I had just finished squeezing my leg into the left boot when my toes knocked against something. Thinking it was a spider or some other horrible animal, I squeaked and tore it off, falling over backward in the process and hitting my head on the bottom shelf of our mystery display. Two books toppled over and fell onto my nose. Edges first, of course.

Now I have a) a grazed toe, b) a bump on the back of my head, and c) a dark blue bruise on my nose (and it's not small, let me tell you!).

The customers are fascinated and get distracted whenever I talk to them. If it was Halloween, I would blend in with the crowd. As it's spring . . . maybe I should set up a Monster Night, so it will look as if I did it on purpose. Or start wearing a mask. I tried to tell John about it today, hoping for adequate compassion (My poor darling! Shall I come and make it better?), but he was kind of short on the phone. I think he took you and Gerry to that posh seafood restaurant with the priceless view across the bay. Every guide mentions it, but I forgot the name. Hope you enjoy it, but think of your blue-nosed friend every now and then, will you?

I'll grab a bowl of cereal in my trailer later as I don't feel like facing the crowds in the supermarket today with my devastating nose.

Karen

P.S. John said you're a lot of fun to have around, and he's thinking about welcoming total strangers more often. How's that for a compliment?

P.P.S. How's Brad? You never mention him.

Dear Karen,

I'm so sorry to hear about your nose. Did you see a doctor? Maybe you should, if it's as big and blue as that?

I'm having such a fabulous time and still wonder why you hesitated for ages before coming here. I'm not sure how you could mistake John for someone who'd steam-roll over you. He's a great man.

I really have to stop now. We're going on a day trip to the mountains!

Leslie

Dear Leslie,

I read your e-mail twice, especially the part where you say you can't understand my shilly-shallying, now that you know John. But you see, he himself was never the problem. I was drawn to him soon enough, and I think every female with eyes in her head would be too. Bound to.

The problem was—is—the rest. All the ramifications. I was happy with Rob at first too. He's a good man, and I thought I would be happy with him forever. But after one year I had lost my soul. It's funny, I still remember my feelings exactly, but I don't know anymore how it came about. It crept in until I was swamped. But why?

To come back to more mundane matters. I have a blister on my foot because of my new sandals, which I thought were ter-ribly chic but which proved to be terribly uncomfortable in-stead, and the delivery of the latest Annabel Grandini didn't arrive as promised today. This in turn caused Mrs. Bluebottle to stomp me into the ground until my remains were as fine as ashes.

So don't blow my way—I might scatter beyond repair.
Karen

Dear Karen,

We've just returned from a trip to the Cascade Mountains. I've never seen such amazing scenery! You should have been with us; then you could describe it. I just don't have that knack for making it come alive. Look at the pictures, and you'll get an idea! I'm so happy.

Leslie

Karen, is everything all right? I haven't heard from you.
Leslie

Dear Leslie,

Yes, I got your e-mail about your wonderful weekend at the Cascade Mountains. Sorry for not replying earlier; I'm busy at the store.

Otherwise, I can report nothing new from this side of the States.

Karen

Dear Leslie,

I don't think I'll ever send this e-mail, but I got so much into the habit of pouring out my heart to you that I can't seem to stop writing, even if it's not fit to send.

I feel lonely tonight. John just talked to me for ten minutes today. Though I have to admit, I had to cut him short because of Mrs. Bluebottle, who needed help with her choice of a romance, as the latest Annabel Grandini has STILL not arrived.

But he could have called again later. And didn't. Anyway.

You two seem to spend so much time together. And you sound over the moon about him. As he does about you.

It seems like a perfect match.

Only, where do I come in? Or rather, come out?

I thought he was serious about us.

Oh, God. I feel so stupid. You're my best friend. I shouldn't even start to think that you could take John away from me. It makes me feel dirty . . . and gives me the feeling I'm a lousy friend.

But I can't get the thought out of my mind. I mean, every soap opera plays out this theme over and over—is that because it's such a heartrending topic, or is it because it happens all the time in real life? I wish I knew.

I'm sitting here, with crossed legs on my bed, staring at the snapshot of you at the Space Needle until it hurts. Though, truth to say, it hurts right away.

Maybe I'm being stupid. It's probably because my nose throbs with pain. Not to mention my blister.

Maybe it's the moon's fault. Full or new moon, I never remember which is supposed to make you depressed, and I can't check because it's cloudy tonight.

I think I'll go to bed now and will not allow a single stupid thought (or any at all, since I can't discern them tonight) to enter my head.

Thank God I have a full supply of M&M's to snuggle up with.

Good night.

Karen

Dear Karen,

I've got a big request, and somehow I never seem to be able to get you on the phone. Do you think I could stay longer? I just love being here, and so I thought I'd stay another week. Please tell me the truth—how are the tourists this year? Do you think you could manage?

Gerry's band came together in John's house this week-end. I was invited too (they said it was a special in-house concert for me!)—it was hilarious. So much fun!

Have to run! We're going on a whale-watching tour, and I know I'll love it from your description!

Leslie

Dear Leslie,

Yes, of course you can stay for another week in Seattle. I can manage the tourists. Those who are kept waiting are happy feasting their eyes on my nose until it's their turn, because then they have to politely avert their gaze.

You haven't said anything about my cloud-display idea. Do you like it? I could ask Rob to build it.

He walked into the store today. I had forgotten how kind he is—and how unassuming. We chatted a bit, and I told him about my idea for the display. He immediately offered to build it if I would paint it. What do you think?

I thought I would feel awkward around him forever after our divorce, but it's funny, when we started talking, it was like old times. Tell me what you think!

Glad to hear Gerry's band came to stay and did a special in-house concert for you. John said it was nice to have someone around, even if it wasn't the one who'd landed him with the whole thing. He said you made up for my loss.

It sounds as if you're having a lot of fun.

My nose is developing a green rim around the edges. Very attractive. A boy (five, six years old?) bounced into the store today. He reminded me of Gerry because of his freckles, but—alas—he does not have the dimples.

With balled fists in his pockets, he stared at me as if I was installed there for the sole purpose of scaring kids away. Finally he said, "Your nose is black."

"I know," I gravely replied.

"Did someone punch you?"

"Yes." I grabbed the offending mystery novel and held it out to him. "This is the culprit."

His eyes widened. "You fight with books?"

"Hmm. Kind of."

He nodded and skipped away.

Later, I heard him say to his grandmother: "The woman in that store fights with her books, Granny. Isn't that weird?" (By the way, his "Granny" is Mrs. Grant, the one who belongs to the same quilting circle as your mother.)

Do you mind very much if we get a fighting reputation? Maybe, in doing so, I'll turn the store into an attraction, and we'll boost sales all across the US. I could hang some books from the ceiling and affix claws on them, so they'll seem to be jumping at you. Hmm. Maybe for Halloween.

Have to go now. We got four crates of books today, and they're blocking the way to the coffee machine.

Karen

Dear Karen,

Mrs. Grant is nice, and I know her grandchild. He's a sweet kid.

Did I tell you I'm so happy here? Seattle is a wonderful place, and that's not nearly saying enough. In a rush . . .

Leslie

Dear Leslie,

This is another letter destined to never reach its goal.

I'm so unhappy. My talks with John are getting shorter and shorter. I know it's due to me, not him, but the words get stuck in my throat whenever he calls, and all I can think of is if he's in love with you. I couldn't blame him.

You know how to flirt, and you're so attractive, with your teasing eyes and your long hair. Compared to you, I'm a block of wood. So serious. So complicated. So reluctant to commit.

Maybe you bowled him over. It can happen.

In the e-mails I do send off to you, I only write about the stuff I CAN mention, but the things that matter are hidden deep down inside. They hurt more and more every day, and I have to write them down somewhere, because otherwise they will fester on and on and drive me nuts.

Whenever you write (and you don't write much, do you?), you sound intoxicated with happiness and love. I didn't write much when I was in Seattle either. Was too busy . . . as you seem to be. Oh, God.

When you told me you wanted to prolong your vacation, something cold swished through my body and froze me to the spot.

Darn.

I wish I knew what to do.

Karen

Dear Leslie,

The boy came back today. He inspected my nose, then informed me that a) the green rim is widening, and that b) his name is Ben.

Introductions performed, he asked me to teach him how to fight with a book. It seems he tried it last night and found them unworthy opponents.

I said that in order to have a good fight with a book, you have to learn the technique, and (as the store was empty) I was just demonstrating it, flat on my back, holding the mystery at an angle above me, when Mrs. Bluebottle stomped in and fell over me.

She got the impression I had fainted.

What does a good citizen do when she falls over a fainted bookstore owner?

Right on.

She clutches her magnificent bosom and shouts for help. She did it so well, traffic stopped on the street outside, and about fifteen people came charging into our store, staring at me.

I should have put up that note after all, the one that tells you what to do when finding me unconscious.

I sat up, waved my book, and said, "I'm fine. Don't worry, guys."

Mrs. Bluebottle considered my obvious health a personal insult and asked me in a voice that chilled even my black-green-rimmed nose what on earth I thought I was doing on the floor.

"I was just executing a special demonstration," I replied with dignity, and I dusted off my bottom.

Ben had the time of his life and told his mother I reminded him of Batman.

I didn't dare ask why.

Karen

P.S. You don't write much lately. Do tell me what you think about the display, will you? Rob came in again today and showed me a great drawing of what he could do.

Dear Leslie,

Thank you for your message on the answering machine. I'm sorry I missed you; I had gone out to buy M&M's. My stock had reached a dangerously low level, and I really had to do something about it to avert a crisis, particularly as Ben has made it a habit to drop in and diminish them at an alarming rate.

I'm glad you like the idea of the cloud display. Yes, of course it means I will go to Rob's house. He can hardly build it in the main aisle, wedged between the *New York Times* best sellers and the kids' books. But don't worry, it'll be fine.

Glad to hear you'll take another day trip to the Cascade Mountains. It's something we didn't get around to doing when I was there. Say hi to John from me.

Karen

Dear Leslie,

Just a short note to tell you that our earnings this month exceed any previous May! Maybe I should hit myself on the nose more often. Will go to Rob's house tonight. He said he has almost finished the display and that we have to discuss a few details. Will send you a picture soon.

Karen

P.S. Forgot to hit the Send button earlier. Have just come back. Time at Rob's was wonderful. He cooked dinner for me (chicken breasts with vegetables—how's that?), and we sat in his kitchen for ages, talking. The air was soft tonight, like a caress. I wonder why he has never found himself another woman.

Dear Leslie,

I miss John. I miss him. I miss him. It hurts so much, even M&M's don't help. I only told you in my earlier e-mail (the one I did send) that the evening at Rob's place was great.

Which is true.

But at the same time a big hollow inside me got larger and larger every minute until I thought I would burst into tears.

Rob is so solid.

So stolid.

Of course he's kind—oh, so kind that I feel like a criminal for not having stayed with him. But we don't even share the same sense of humor! I had forgotten all about it until I made a joke tonight—and he was offended. I felt propelled back to the last days of our marriage, when nothing I did or said arrived at his ears the way I meant it.

And whenever I mentioned things I want to do, places I want to see, he shook his head as if I was an impatient child planning how to become Mr. President or the Director of the Bombastic Circus (founded by yours truly). Suddenly, with that shake of his head, I was transported back in time. It came like a rush, and I knew again why I thought I had lost my soul before our divorce. He always wanted to rein me in, to curb my temper and my lust for life. He didn't do it with anything drastic; he just shook his head and smiled that little condescending smile. Tonight he asked if I still liked my gypsy life, making me feel as if I was a child in a bad phase of independence-seeking but that he was sure it would soon be over and that I would behave like an adult one day soon.

It exasperated me, but now, with a few years' distance, I'm able to see his good qualities. He could be a wonderful husband—just not for me.

I was so glad when I was on my way home, with the night air coming through the open window, caressing my skin, making me tingle with pleasure. I felt released.

John would have understood. He would have glanced at me in that soul-seeing way of his, and he would have known.

I'm so unhappy.

A teenager with blue hair and a piercing in her belly button forgot a magazine on the counter today. The headline caught my attention—*My Best Friend Stole My Lover*—and the next thing I knew, I grabbed up the tabloid and gobbled down the whole article without once looking up. They say a woman should fight. They say she should make it clear she is not a doormat.

Oh, well. It's not that I don't like to fight.

I do fight if it's absolutely unavoidable.

But I had my doubts about John and me all along (or, rather, our future), and now, if he has fallen in love with you and you with him, and if you're so happy, particularly after the disaster with Matthew last year that broke your heart, then how can I make a scene, if before I had always tried to keep John at arm's length? It's not logical, and if even I can see it, it's pretty obvious.

Though you have exactly the same problem I do, come to think of it. But you won't fret around; you'll certainly find a solution quickly. And I bet you would manage such a momentous change in your life without touching our store either. That's something I just couldn't figure out—how to continue with our store and my skiing life if I committed to John. You, however, will manage it somehow.

Why, oh, why did you fall in love with John? I mean, I can't blame you, having done it myself, but I wish it wasn't true. I'll send this e-mail into the ether too and tell myself that this time next year I'll be happy again. I hope.

Karen

Dear Karen,

I'm sorry I haven't written for so long, but things have been in a whirl over here. I've tried to reach you on the phone, but we never seem to find a quiet minute; that's why I finally thought I would send my big question via e-mail. So here we go. I'd like to sell my part in our bookstore.

Um. That's it. What do you think?

Leslie

Dear Leslie,

When I got your e-mail this morning, I didn't trust my eyes. I shut down the computer and started it again, then lowered myself carefully back onto my bed, clutched my first cup of coffee, and cautiously reopened Outlook. It was still there.

I sat and stared at the screen until my eyes started to water.

Are you seriously asking me what I would say if you sold your part of our store?

Do you have any doubts about my reaction?

I guess you don't; otherwise you would have called. Okay, okay, I know the different time zones make it difficult to find an appropriate moment, and you certainly didn't want to spring your news on me with a line of customers waiting and watching me faint, but honestly!

Besides, you'll be back in two days, so you could have told me personally.

Or won't you?

What on earth is going on? I thought we were both committed to our store. I was thinking only yesterday that whatever happened, you would not touch it. I remember you saying it was the one good and stable thing in your life.

And now that's all gone. Just because you've fallen in love? (Oh, yes, I know, even though you never told me. But I've known you long enough to recognize the signs.) Isn't it a bit premature to rip up all your roots for a guy you hardly know? I can't believe it.

All day long I trudged through our store with a numb feeling, aware of every detail, as if seeing it for the first time.

The scarred patch next to the coffee machine where you dropped the Christmas candle because you were so giddy from the punch.

The sign on the fridge, saying, *Remember the deal: six bags of M&M's max.*

The huge key to the front door, because you felt an antique lock would give you such a respectable feeling.

The high-tech security bolt on the inside of the door you ordered to make me feel better.

The hideous lilac wall you wanted as a backdrop for the fairy-tale books.

Is all of that unimportant?

Karen

Chapter Eight

Dear Leslie,

They say bad things never come singly. I won't send this e-mail, but all our customers are out at the beach this morning, and I have to get it off my chest. Just as I careened to the store in a kind of shell-shock this morning, my head still reeling from your news, I stumbled over Rob at the doorstep, who seemed to have spent the night there, just to ask me if I didn't want to marry him again. As if mornings were a time to discuss serious things. He should have known better after all the unhappy mornings we shared. I stared at him and opened my mouth to say, "If you were the last man on earth, I wouldn't marry you again." Then, just as the words were on my tongue, something stopped me. He stared at me hopefully like a dog that expects to be patted on the head. I tried to cushion my refusal in soft words, but my head was in a whirl, and nothing soft came out, just bits and pieces that had no business coming out at that point. That I love John, for example. And that you want to sell our store. Then I just stared at him, helpless, and silently opened and closed my mouth like a fish without water.

Rob looked at me, then touched my arm and said, "Think about it. I'll be back." Then he turned to go. I was so relieved.

I won't mail this. My life is getting too complicated.

Karen

Dear Leslie,

I'm sorry I sent such a hateful e-mail. I just cracked up.

If that's what you want to do . . . truly and really, and if you have thought about it for some time, then of course I won't stand in your way.

Only, you know I don't have enough money to buy your share. We'll have to work out some solution, only I can't think about one right now.

Please excuse me for lashing out earlier.

Karen

Dear Karen,

I think we should talk on the phone. Tonight, at 9, all right?

Leslie

Dear Leslie,

It's been two days since you sent me your message, and I still can't believe you want to sell out. Our talk on the phone tonight didn't make it any better. We were both tongue-tied and awkward, and that was so strange, it suffocated me.

My whole world is upside down.

I don't know what to do or feel.

I don't even know if I can trust you anymore, seeing that you want to pull out of our business. If anybody had told me that two weeks ago, I would have laughed in his face.

I'm a fool, wondering if I can trust you, for heaven's sake, after you have taken away John already. I should have cut up our friendship long ago.

And in spite of all, here I am, sitting on my bed as usual, writing long e-mails to you like a demented puppy that can't remember anything but the one thing it has been trained to do: Write to Leslie, pour out your heart.

Only Leslie isn't there anymore to read it.

She has fallen in love with the man I love.

My head hurts from thinking about it all day long. I'm afraid I snapped at Mrs. Bluebottle, who pointedly asked when you would return. For a minute I thought I would burst into tears right there and then.

Ben came, and after inhaling half a package of M&M's, he peered at me with an expert eye and said, "Why are you angry?"

And I couldn't hold on to myself and said, "Oh, my best friend is going out with the man I love, and on top of that, she wants to sell our store, but otherwise, everything's fine."

As soon as the words were out of my mouth, I regretted saying them. Gosh, don't I have anybody else to confide in but a six-year-old?

It seems I don't. I wish my mother was still alive so I could get some comfort there.

On second thought, maybe not.

She would say I never should have trusted a man. That's where heartbreak comes from. "Yes," she would say with that tight smile of hers, "you should have known better." After all, she told me often enough.

Ben stuffed a green M&M into his mouth and nodded as if he was used to receiving staggering confidences from grown-ups. "I can marry you," he finally offered between a yellow and a red M&M.

What a sacrifice.

It was the only time that day I managed a smile.

Just as I closed the store for the night, things got worse.

Rob was standing outside, waiting for me to come out. Have I told you he has finished the display and that I painted it yesterday night? It looks great.

Sorry, I forgot you couldn't care less. Won't mention it again.

When I saw his calm, kind face, something strange happened. I felt so much in need of a friend that, for one instant, I forgot the truth that had been hammered into me during two miserable years of marriage; I forgot that we would never share the same dreams; I just knew he would always be a harbor I could run to. All the pent-up emotions inside me rushed out, and I catapulted myself into his arms and clung to him.

He caught me and held me close, and for a second I felt better, but then he started to kiss me, and suddenly I realized that that would never do.

I'm such a louse. Such a weak louse. How could I take advantage of him, when I knew I would never want more than a hug?

I eased away from him and averted my face, and just as I did so, I glimpsed the back of a man hurrying away from us, and I could have sworn it was John.

John, who's supposed to be in Seattle.

John, whom I miss so much, it hurts as if someone has torn out a part of me.

I stared and stared and opened my mouth to shout, but only a croak came out. The guy marched to a Jeep parked at the curb, swung himself inside, and roared off without once looking back.

A Jeep.

John loves Jeeps, heaven knows why.

It can't have been John, can it?

John has loads of work to do.

He has no time for quick trips across the whole country.

Certainly not.

Most definitely not.

It must have been a trick of the eye. When you're in love, everybody looks like the person you miss, right? Everybody reminds you of him, even the most unlikely people. That must have been it.

I had a hard time explaining to Rob that it was all a misunderstanding. I think he believes I'm playing with him, and I also think he's disgusted with my behavior. He has a right to feel that way. I'm so ashamed of myself. If he decides never to talk to me again, I wouldn't blame him.

Am going to delete this message now. For once, it didn't help to write it all down.

How I miss John! He hasn't called today.

Karen

Dear Karen,

I only get the voice mail whenever I call. Please get in touch, and tell me what you think about my staying out here longer.

Leslie

Dear Leslie,

I'm sorry I missed your call; I was in front of the store, filling the cloud display. Rob put hidden wheels underneath, so I can roll it in and out, depending on the weather.

Yes, I can manage another three days on my own. But if you plan any more postponements, please tell me now, so I can try to find a replacement for you.

I'm not sure if I got your message right, so I repeated it three times. It still didn't make sense.

How can you have thought I would be "sort of relieved" about your decision to sell the store? What on earth did you think I would do? Burst into song?

Am confused.

Write soon.
Karen

Dear Leslie,

I wish I didn't have the urge to write to you. I'm probably in denial about the whole thing, and that's why I continue exactly the way I do. Pitiable, really.

John hasn't called me today. I guess he feels bad about exchanging me for you. I don't blame him. I wouldn't have the gall to talk to me either. Or maybe it *was* him yesterday night, and he thinks I'm two-timing him. What an incredible muddle.

I should talk to him. My hand dialed his number about forty times but without touching the phone. What would I say anyway? That I miss him? That I wish it had been different?

That I despise him?

You know, it's funny. I don't despise him. Nor do I despise you. I'm just sad for myself. And tired. So tired. I wish I hadn't gone to Seattle. I believed in our love when I was there. But as soon as I returned, reality jumped in, and it got lost . . . that special feeling I've never had before . . . it just got lost.

Darn.

Why did my mother have to be right?

Karen

Dear Leslie,

You're back.

And you've never been so far away from me before.

It feels as if I'm working next to a stranger. Gone are the times when we laughed ourselves silly about one thing or other. It's just business, and even that isn't as relaxed as it used to be.

We're barely talking and creep around each other as if afraid to touch.

I'm so unhappy. Every time you're on the phone, talking to

John, I feel sick. If only you didn't call him "Snoodle" all the time. What kind of a nickname is that anyway?

I've not talked to him even once since you've gotten back, as you're so busy jumping at the phone as soon as it rings. And it rings quite a lot. But then, I'm not keen to answer it anyway.

And you know what? You look gorgeous. Your eyes shine, and your skin is smooth like cream. Ben asked me if you were a star on television. How's that for a compliment?

I feel like a dried-up beetle next to you all the time. Really, it's not fair to look like that. I'm not sure I can stand it much longer.

You know, I'd never have thought so, but I'm looking forward to splitting up. At least I thought so, until Mr. Greenway showed up today, strutting around as if he wanted to buy the Rockefeller Building and not just a tiny bookstore in Southampton. Every time his arrogant gaze skimmed over the shelves, I wanted to grab the books, hold them to my chest, and cry, "They're mine, all mine! You won't get them!"

Instead, I smiled and nodded and prayed that he wouldn't get stuck to our latest superglued noose. I thought I would faint when he stopped with his left foot right on top and started to hold a monologue for three endless minutes, making snotty remarks about the minuscule crack in the wall that has been there for ages, disturbing nobody. All at once I felt very protective about our crack and exchanged a glance with you, and, for a minute, everything between us was the way it used to be. Before you decided to sell out.

I hate the buyers!

All of them.

Every time I gaze out at the ocean, I feel like crying because I might have to leave soon and won't see this view ever again.

Every time I stub my toe on that stupid crooked slab in the sidewalk, I feel like kneeling and kissing it, knowing I won't be around much longer to be annoyed by it.

I think I'm getting a bit carried away. But what the heck?

If only I had the money to buy your share, Leslie.

But even if I did, it wouldn't help, as I don't think I could leave the store unattended all winter. And I wouldn't want to live here in the dark months either. It's so gray. I would miss my blue mountains so much.

I'm in a sorry state. Even M&M's don't help anymore.

I'll stop whining now. Will delete this maudlin stuff and lift my head. Tomorrow I'll try to build myself a future.

Tomorrow.

Karen

Dear Leslie,

When you asked me if you could fly back to Seattle for another four days, I felt like jumping up and down in frustration and banging something over your head. How can your priorities shift so much so fast? But just as I opened my mouth to say there's no way I can handle the crowds on my own, you touched my arm and said that bit about my becoming your maid of honor.

It's a wonder I didn't faint.

I had no clue you wanted to get married like lightning. You, of all people! You never wanted to be bound by any shackles. You always said we should keep things fluffy and fun. Those were your very words. And now you go and get married? With four weeks' notice? I mean . . . hello?

But worse, I've never heard of a woman who plans to marry your ex-lover inviting you to become her maid of honor. Every instinct that's responsible for self-preservation should scream inside you.

I can't believe it's you, Leslie.

At least you can still read my face. Though, truth to tell, anybody would have read my face at that moment, even Mrs. Bluebottle.

So you just turned around and left me standing there, speechless, because that darn phone rang again, and you talked for ages to "Snoodle" . . . and I wonder if it might have been better to let you go.

Karen

Dear Leslie,

I've done it. I told you to go and take those four days off. And you've left like a shot, so at least the phone has stopped ringing, and I work like a machine gone into overdrive, and it's the best I can do, as it leaves me too tired to think about anything when I finally come home to my trailer.

Hope you enjoy your days with "Snoodle."

Karen

Leslie,

I found your official wedding invitation in the mail today.

Ripped open the creamy, thick envelope with a sick lurch of the heart, and then . . . then I stared and stared and stared.

The words blurred in front of my eyes, and I had to blink like crazy to get them into focus again.

You are cordially invited to celebrate the wedding of Leslie Carter and Brad Housten . . .

Brad.

Brad??!!

I staggered out of the shop and sat on the steps, putting my head onto my knees.

"Is that another way to fight with books?" Ben's voice asked me, enthusiastic to learn a new maneuver.

"No," I replied, "it's a way to avoid being sick."

I thought you had fallen in love with John.

You never stopped talking about him. And he praised you to the sky!

Brad Housten was never even mentioned once.

Never even once, I repeat.

And your stupid habit of calling him Snoodle didn't exactly help.

I'm so ashamed. I don't believe I can call you. I think I have to compose a careful e-mail. Oh, how embarrassing. What a fool I am.

But . . . but why did John stop calling me? Why?

I'll go down to the jetty and cool my feet. And calm myself. And eat a bag or two of M&M's.

And then I'll write a sensible e-mail to you. One I will send, for a change.

Oh, God.

Karen

Dear Leslie,

I have to admit something I'm not proud of, and I hope you'll understand.

I think it was that shot of you, John, and Gerry in front of the Space Needle that did it. And the way John said you were so much fun to have around. And . . . well, I'm afraid I'm not being very lucid.

Right.

I'll start again.

In all your e-mails to me, you never mentioned Brad, not even once. You didn't, I swear it! I rechecked all your e-mails, and you don't even talk about him in passing. So what was I supposed to think, eh?

God. There's no way to do this right. I have to spring it on you. I thought you were going out with John.

Not Brad.

When I got your wedding invitation, I was flabbergasted.

Are you sure you're going to marry Brad?
Quite sure?
Karen

Dear Leslie,

I'm sitting here on my bed, crying and laughing at the same time. Talking to you on the phone just now felt as if I'd found a long-lost friend. Which is exactly what happened.

I'm so glad you understood your VSF (that's short for *Very Stupid Friend*), and you may refer to me that way whenever there's company around. Otherwise, feel free to use the long version.

I would never have thought you could be reluctant to tell me about Brad!

Of course I said all those nasty things about him. But that was fifteen years ago, and I was cold and sitting in a muddy tent, and you behaved as if we had just arrived on some sort of golden cloud, for crying out loud!

And when I wrote about the night of meeting him at Gerry's concert, of course I said that thing about not so much hair, but that doesn't mean he's repulsive! In fact, I thought he was really attractive once I got a good, not-so-mud-stained look at him.

You shouldn't have hesitated to tell me he's your One and Only. And you shouldn't have felt embarrassed about throwing all your much-preached principles of keeping it light overboard and getting "shackled for life." That's not like you, Leslie.

Okay, okay, I admit, I'm not exactly in a position to reproach you for holding back.

You're perfectly right, of course: I should have made a scene when I suspected you of "taking" John away. I should have thrown a pile of books at you, to make your nose match mine—or worse. It would have saved us so much heartbreak (even if it would have created havoc with our inventory).

I don't know why I didn't.

I've wondered about it myself, now that my head is not quite so fuzzy anymore. I think it's partly because I didn't dare to believe in my luck—and John's love. (Yup, my mother talking, you're right.) It's true what they say—you forge your own destiny. I didn't believe in my happiness, and so I destroyed it.

But, in my defense, I had another reason to withhold throwing the aforementioned books. I don't believe in anybody having the power to "take" your lover away. John is a free person with his own mind. It's not as if our relationship had reached a difficult stage or had gone stale either. So I thought (in some subconscious recess of my mind) that if he wanted you, it wouldn't help if I worked against it. Am not sure if you get my drift. Sounds kind of confused. Well, it IS a bit. Confused, I mean.

And partly it was because I wanted you to be happy, after last year and all you have been through with Matthew. You do look radiant, you know. (Ain't I noble? I can hardly believe it myself.)

Oh, by the way. I forgot to tell you. I'm honored to be your maid of honor. Glowing pink around the edges, in fact.

As long as you don't put me into some sort of scratchy lilac tulle dress, the way Rosemary did. I will never forget how we scratched each other in the bathroom until our backs were bright red, clashing with the lilac.

I have to call John now and explain.

Do you recall the time when we were about to take our finals in math, standing shivering in front of the classroom, and I said this was the lowest point in my life, as low as it could get, and you replied—totally unruffled, I might add—that there would come a time in our life when we would love to retake this exam instead of doing whatever it was that life would throw at us?

I didn't want to believe it at the time.

I preferred not to.

But if someone waved a math exam right about now, I would choose it.

Gladly.

Think of me! Please.

Karen

Dear Karen,

Don't put off the call; get on the phone right away. John's a great man, and he knows how much you had to fight to get rid of your mother's heritage.

I'll keep my fingers crossed for you. Call me, and tell me ALL the minute you hang up! I want you to be happy. As happy as I am.

I'm so glad we talked! I felt awful all the time when I thought you were angry with me because I wanted to sell my share in the store. I never even IMAGINED that you thought anything else. But you always looked at me with such a disappointed expression in your eyes that I didn't feel like sharing anything about Brad.

Besides, even I found it hard to admit that I had thrown all my lifelong principles overboard and had decided to get married without once looking back on "keep it light and fluffy." I think we were both too busy with ourselves, but thank God that's over. I'm so glad we're friends again. Now go and call John. I'm thinking of you!

Leslie

P.S. Snoodle is NOT a silly nickname. It's lovely.

Dear Leslie,

It was worse than I thought.

Worse than I could ever have imagined.

John answered the phone the first time it rang and said in a curt voice, "Can I call you back in an hour? I've got a meeting I can't interrupt right now."

I deflated like a pricked balloon. Just as I had worked myself up to render a comprehensible apology! I had even memorized my first sentence, so it would launch me right into the middle of the matter and avoid any stammer or stutter.

Have I ever told you that he once said to his secretary to always, always put me right through, even if he was busy? It seems that time is over now.

I didn't think I could feel any worse before the call, but those two short sentences did it.

He called me one endless hour and twelve minutes later. I forgot my launching sentence the minute I heard his voice and served up some mixed hash that didn't make any sense at all.

He listened in silence.

When I ran out of stupid things to say, he finally asked, in a voice totally devoid of feeling, "Do I get it right that you thought I'd had a love affair with Leslie?"

"Er. Yes."

"You must have a high opinion of me."

"No! I mean, yes." I broke out in a sweat.

"You know something, Karen?"

"What?"

"It takes two to build a relationship. Up to now, all you've done is run away and allege that I had an affair with your best friend. Without ever mentioning it to me, if I may say so. That gives me the feeling you're doing your utmost to find reasons not to commit to our relationship."

I opened my mouth, but nothing came out. He's so right.

John had already swept on, still in that controlled voice: "Besides, you made it a habit to cut short my phone calls, and when I came to talk to you, all the way to Long Island, I had to watch you throwing yourself into another man's arms."

Oh, God. Oh, God. So it *had* been John that day! If only I hadn't hugged Rob.

"Well, Karen? Is there anything you wish to say to me?"

"I . . . I . . . it wasn't the way it seemed to be." The second the words were out of my mouth, I wished I had shot myself rather than use exactly the same cliché every stupid guy says when caught red-handed.

I got the reply I deserved.

"I see." His voice chilled me.

A painful pause froze the connection between us.

Finally he said, "Anything else?"

I remained dumb. Everything I could say would sound like a subterfuge.

"No, John. Nothing," I finally whispered and hung up.

Karen

WHAT? You threw yourself into Rob's arms? When? Why? What did I miss???

Leslie

Dear Leslie,

Yeah, I admit, I kind of threw myself into Rob's arms.

I forgot you didn't know. When we weren't talking, I got into the habit of writing sham e-mails to you that I never sent; that's why I thought I'd told you already.

But I only hugged Rob once! And just for a minute. Or even less. It happened after I learned that you wanted to sell the store, and I was badly in need of comfort. But as soon as I got there (into his arms, I mean), I realized what a mistake I was making and jumped away again. But by then, John had whipped around. I even saw his back before he roared off in his rented Jeep. Can you imagine?

Can't write more. Am too depressed.

Karen

P.S. You know what's the worst? John is right. It's all my own fault.

Dear Karen,

God, you really made a mess of this one. We met John yesterday, and I made a point of saying something nice about you, but his eyes looked like some sort of hard stone (what is it you always say—quartz?), and I'm afraid I lost track of what I'd been saying. He's quite formidable when angry, isn't he?

I've no clue how we can get you out of this! I feel all limp and spent just thinking about it. But I'll keep on thinking. We have to come up with something.

Leslie

Dear Leslie,

I think there's just one way to solve this. Would you mind very much tending the store on your own when you return? Just for a few days. I need to go to Seattle and talk to John to sort it all out. I can't explain it on the phone.

I know I'm asking a lot, and I brought it all on myself, but I simply can't face another phone conversation with John like the one yesterday. I tried to compose an e-mail to him, but it all sounded self-righteous and stupid, and I just need to be there in person.

Karen

P.S. The only time I smiled today was at the jetty. I sat there for an hour and tried to get my special "blue" feeling again, to take away some of the pain. But it eluded me, though the air touched me, warm and soft, smelling of hay and tang.

I think it's easier to be a martyr than a fool. At least as a martyr, it isn't your own fault. And you have a saintly feeling on top, which the fool most decidedly hasn't. Believe me, I know what I'm talking about.

All at once something creaked on the boards behind me and scared me so much, I almost fell into the water. When I looked over my shoulder, Ben jumped back and shouted from a distance, "Have you had chicken pox?"

"Yes," I said, and then I saw it. His face was covered with about a million red spots.

"I'm not allowed out," he said with a glint in his eye and a broad grin. "But it's so boring inside, and I saw you sitting here, and, besides, I think all the old people have had chicken pox already; I just have to be careful of the kids."

"Sure," I said. "Come sit beside me."

Which he did. He told me about the fish he caught last week and about the new sister he got some weeks ago ("It would have been better if it had been a boy, but Mom says she can't exchange it, only I think she could have tried harder"), and all at once he stopped and peered at me sideways and said, "You're sad."

Really, this kid is almost on a par with John in soul-searching matters!

He wrinkled his freckled and spotted nose like some benighted guru and said, "You know how I know? You look like Granny when my granddad died."

Lovely comparison.

"It's because I was stupid," I explained. "I love somebody very much, but I didn't believe in it, and that's why I destroyed it. And it's all my own fault."

He nodded. "Like when I washed my crocodile, and all the stuffing came out, and Mom said I shouldn't have done it, only I thought it would be all right because a crocodile lives in the water, doesn't it?"

That was when I smiled. "Yeah. Just like that," I said. "I washed the stuffing out of John."

Fitting image, ain't it?

Karen

Dear Karen,

A catastrophe has hit me. Just as I got your e-mail and prepared for the flight back, two red spots on my chest started to itch. Then I got a temperature, then more red spots, and finally Snoodle took a look at me and informed me that I had chicken pox. He knows . . . he has kids with chicken pox at school all the time. Can you BELIEVE IT?

Ben must have passed them on to me when we shared that bag of M&M's.

I feel so stuck. And I'm so sorry to let you down, just when you need me! Should I send you the medical certificate—or a picture? I look awful!

I dare not think about my wedding. I still haven't convinced the chef to change the dessert to orange mousse, nor do I know how many chairs the lighthouse can provide for the wedding, and what if there's a fog and all our guests fall into the water? Aaaarrgh.

It's a disaster. Snoodle laughs at me, but he doesn't know that the wedding is the smallest problem. He said I shouldn't even try to book a flight, as they would never let me on board. Is that true?

Leslie

Dear Leslie,

Oh, no! I'm so sorry for you! Of course you don't need to send me your medical certificate or a picture of your ravaged face. I believe you. Yes, you must have caught them from Ben before they showed—what incredible bad luck. Brad is right; no airline would take you on as a passenger, with the truth written large across your face, so please don't torture yourself. How on earth did you escape the epidemic waves of chicken pox in kindergarten?

Of course I wish it wasn't now, as I long (and dread) to talk to John. But on the other hand, it's better if you have 'em now than on your wedding day. Imagine!

I'll keep up the shop with the help of Jill. I asked her today, and she said she still knew her way around from the time she helped you at Christmas. So don't worry about it, we'll even manage the Fourth-of-July crowds and the reading of *No More Lies*, though I'll have to think about a less painful way to distract the customers than a green-and-black nose.

I'll even show all prospective buyers around, including Mr. Greenway, who wishes to come again (!). Will do my utmost to charm them all. Have filled the crack in the wall with chewing gum, by the way, and painted it with white nail polish. It's invisible now, and I'm very proud of myself.

And of course I'll discuss the change of dessert with the chef of the catering service for you as tactfully as I can (orange mousse sounds scrumptious), and I will check the number of chairs with the administrator of the lighthouse too.

Don't worry, the weather will be fine, and nobody will get lost in the fog, and no, you won't lose any guests who'll disappear over the cliffs on Montauk Point. We'll organize a festive-looking rope all around the premises, so no danger there.

I think it's wonderful that you will celebrate on Long Island, to say good-bye to everybody before you move off to Seattle. Hmm. I think I'll change the topic now.

But do relax, Leslie. We have more than three weeks to go. You'll be back to your usual gorgeous self by then, not a hint of the red spots left.

Love,
Karen

Dear Karen,

Sorry for not writing earlier, but the chicken pox shook me with an iron grip. Today my temperature is lower, and the spots seem to have stopped multiplying every minute, so I feel a bit more human. (I still don't look it, though.) Snoodle is great. He made chicken soup for me. What a wonderful man.

Did the wedding preparations go all right? I'm so grateful you're covering them, on top of everything else.

Keep up, dear! I'll fly to you the minute the airline lets me get on board.

Leslie

Dear Leslie,

I'm so, so glad to hear you're better. Just don't scratch yourself, or you'll end up with scars!

The orange mousse is on—no problem there. Have arranged sufficient chairs too, and the rope will be installed. Had a talk with God, who promised to send a warm day with a cooling breeze, so all is well.

Oh, God, I just realized: We can't go and buy my dress together! By the time you'll arrive, you'll have too much to do! And leaving it to the last minute will make me a bit nervous. Do you have any special color in mind?

Karen

Dear Karen,

Dark red, like the roses in my bouquet! I leave the rest up to you.

Did you make sure to extend the family's invitation to Ben, the little chicken-pox man?

Leslie

Dear Leslie,

Are you sure you want to invite Ben? I know his granny is in the same quilting group as your mother, but he's a little monster. Yes, yes, he's an endearing little monster, I admit, but are you aware that he'll eat everything in sight? Oh, well, at least it's not a buffet, so he can't create wholesale havoc.

Karen

Yup. Invite him. I fell for those freckles.
Did I tell you what a wonderful friend you are? I'm so glad I can absolutely trust you with the organization of the wedding. Thank you, thank you, thank you!

Leslie

Dear Leslie,

I tried to call John again. Couldn't bear to wait until you're fine. Besides, I have an inkling that the chicken pox–wedding combination will require tight timing, and I might have to stay here until after the wedding.

I called him on his cell as usual, but he must have rerouted it, because I ended talking to Sandra, his secretary. She said, "Hold on a second," and I was just fighting to get some sort of control over my breathing, when she came back on the line and said, "I'm sorry, he must have stepped out of his office. Shall I leave a message?"

I said it wasn't necessary.

You can't get into his office without crossing hers. So there's no chance he can have slipped out without being seen.

He doesn't want to talk to me, Leslie.

On second thought, I won't send this e-mail.

It might make you feel bad.

Karen

P.S. As I won't send it anyway, I might add that Mr. Greenway has made an offer. But he wants the whole shop, not me thrown in as side dish. I told him you're ill and that I can only discuss his offer with you in August (I added your wedding and the honeymoon into my calculations). Now he thinks you're going through a life-threatening operation. Ahhh.

I should discuss this with you right now, I know, but you sound so desperately grateful already that you would say no to him just to please me, even though it might be the best offer we can get. As I'm not yet ready to say nay or yea either (it scares the living daylights out of me!), I played for time.

Chapter Nine

Dear Karen,

You were right. I'll only be able to get on board a plane the day before the wedding. The doctor told me today. I feel awful.

Leslie

Dear Leslie,

Don't feel awful. You can't help it! Today I have to keep it short because I'm galloping at full speed, stretched out to my full length, with my belly touching the ground.

Here's the news—to save time, in bullet points, not in prose:

Kate and Jerry are delighted to accept your invitation. Who are they? Do I have to place them close to your mother or far away?

Kerry (your cousin, not Brad's grandmother) says she can't bring Bob but will bring Spotty instead. Is that her dog or her current lover?

The caterer informed me that the orange mousse might be

difficult due to some strike in Spain, if I got it right, and asks if lemon mousse would be fine too. Don't lemons come from Spain as well? Or is it Florida? I told him I would discuss it with you, but, seeing as he's such a competent man, I expected him to find oranges from somewhere else. Even if the Spanish oranges are the best, there are others around, and I would trust him implicitly to make everything perfect for you. I suggested Brazil, Florida, and California, as if I knew anything about it. He grew an inch, pushed back his hair, and said he would pull a few strings. So keep your fingers crossed for the oranges. I think I'll have to force myself to test it beforehand :-). The way he's acting, he might have mislaid the recipe.

Gosh, I wanted to be short and concise. And what happens? I talk for ages about orange mousse.

I vow to get better.

Right.

Next point:

I found a dress.

It's long (of course).

It's simple (oh, yes).

Until I move. Then a slit opens at one side that makes me feel even sexier than when I wear my high boots.

It's made of raw silk, just like your dress, but mine is a deep, deep red, matching the roses in your bouquet, as requested.

I'm so glad you're not forcing me into one of those petticoat things that make me look like a cross between Miss Piggy and a kangaroo.

The administrator at the lighthouse has asked me to tell everybody that they shouldn't throw rice or confetti over you, because the wind takes it to the ocean, and it causes sickness among the fish. They have so many weddings, it has become quite an issue.

I pondered that problem for a while and then had a brilliant idea. I bought ten drums of fish food (the finest you can get), so the guests can throw the stuff over you. Hope you approve.

You can see, I'm throwing myself into this wedding thing wholeheartedly.

Have you invited John?

Karen

Dear Karen,

Yes, I invited John and Gerry ages ago, simply because they were with us at the Cascade Mountains when IT happened . . . and also because they more or less brought us together. Do you want me to dis-invite them? I think they've booked their flights already.

Leslie

Dear Leslie,

No, of course not! I quite understand. You can't dis-invite them now; it would be so impolite. I'll have to find time for my talk with John sometime when he's over here, then. After the ceremony, of course. Don't worry—no scenes at your wedding. I'll make a note with that command on it and will stick it inside my handbag, so I'll see it every time I open it to take out my dainty handkerchief to dry my tears.

Well.

So John will be here.

It'll save me the trip to Seattle.

God.

I'm so nervous.

Only a few more days. The spots will fade soon—don't panic.

Karen

P.S. It's odd, but I can't sleep lately, though I should be tired by rights.

Dear Leslie,

Your mother just told me half your family is allergic to citrus fruits! Is that true?

Karen

Dear Karen,

Absolutely NOT. She just says so because SHE is allergic to citrus fruits and thinks it's a most interesting ailing. Ignore her.

Leslie

Dear Leslie,

Phew. I'm glad it's only your mother (sorry about the way that sounds). Does she change her allergies often? I ordered chocolate mousse for her and a few more in reserve, in case others want it too when they see it. (Thinking of Ben here—and maybe Gerry.) Okay?

Karen

P.S. Have decided not to reveal the new dessert to your mother. Don't want her to develop a sudden allergy to chocolate.

. . . way to go, girl. I see you know how to handle my mother. Thank you, thank you for everything!

Leslie

Dear Leslie,

Have tested the orange mousse. It's HEAVENLY. Can we order another fifty so I can have second helpings? If I could buy them like M&M's, I would have to change my passion.

Karen

Dear Karen,

Just remembered that I read something when my brain was still riddled with fever but can't find your e-mail anymore. Did you mention dried FISH FOOD instead of confetti?

Leslie

Dear Leslie,

No, of course the dried fish food was a joke. Rely on me. It would indeed have a stingy smack about it. I ordered tiny herrings instead. Fresh, of course.

Karen

. . . are you all right? Not too much stress or anything?
Leslie

Dear Leslie,

Yes, yes, of course I'm all right, thanks for asking.

Everything is working out fine. All under control. Even the tiny herrings in the bathtub.

Will have to buy four pairs of stockings, as the ones I plan to wear are gossamer-thin and threaten to dissolve with a mere look, leaving me with runs so wide, they'll look like firemen-ladders all the way up my legs.

I have heard that someone has long since invented stockings that NEVER snag, but they are withholding the patent, as it would ruin the industry. If I could get my hands on THAT patent! Ha.

Or maybe I should go for the spray-on version they have in the shops now. I've never tried it before and am scared I'll end up glued to my dress or chair.

Oh, Leslie, I'm so nervous. When will John come? Just the night before?

Karen

Dear Karen,

    John has some important business meeting and will only arrive in time for the ceremony. I tried to make him come earlier, but I'm afraid he saw through me and gave me that "stone" look again.

                                        Leslie

Dear Leslie,

Maybe it's a good thing that John and I won't have time to speak before the wedding. I'm so nervous about it. What will I say to him? Maybe I should write down my starting sentence and stick it into my handbag, next to the note that says *Make no scenes*. Only it might look funny if I start rooting around in my handbag the minute he shows up.

Oh, God.

Do you think he'll talk to me?

Maybe he'll ignore me completely?

I placed him at a table across the room from me, so he'll be at a safe distance. He'll have Ben's Granny for company, and I think they'll get along fine, as I have recently discovered her rather wicked sense of humor. She told me in great detail how her older sister (91) and a fluffy-haired friend of hers (89) got into fisticuffs because they were both keen on the same youngster (77) who had just joined the nursing home. There you go. It never ends.

I also put Kerry and Spotty at that table. At least they'll have a good starter to their conversation, asking how Spotty came to have such a nickname! (You'll notice I nobly refrain from asking why you call Brad "Snoodle"!)

Karen

Dear Karen,

    I don't remember inviting a Spotty. Kerry is supposed to come with Bob. Maybe Spotty is Bob's successor?

Can't tell you the Snoodle *background—I had to promise Brad I would NEVER tell anybody.*

Gerry just called and said he wanted to play a special piece for me. Would that be all right for you? I said I'd have to check with you because you're the Master of Ceremonies.

Leslie

Dear Leslie,

You'll almost be on the plane by now, but I hope this e-mail will still reach you!

How nice of Gerry to suggest playing a special piece. Don't worry, I'll be fine. . . . I won't break down in loud sobs in the middle of the piece. Promise. I can always drown them in orange mousse.

Karen

Dear Leslie,

Rob just called and asked if he could bring someone after all. She's called Jenny. Jenny! Do you know any Jenny in the area?

I'm bursting with curiosity!

Karen

Dear Leslie,

When I fixed that last rose in your hair and looked into your eyes, I suddenly felt that an era was coming to an end. One more hour, and you'll be Brad's wife. You'll still be my best friend, but it'll be different. I'll miss you.

I have to go now to welcome the guests at the lighthouse, but before I do so, I wanted to tell you I have accepted the offer from Mr. Greenway this morning because he doubled his previous offer. We'll sign the contract after your return.

Enjoy your honeymoon, my dearest friend.

Karen

Dear Leslie,

You're on your way to Hawaii, but I simply have to tell you all about your wedding, or I'll go bust. You say you were present and therefore don't need to learn about it from me?

Wrong. You were present—that much is true—but since you only gazed at Brad all day and night, you certainly didn't see all there was to see.

I thought I would faint when I discovered that Spotty is indeed a dog. A Dalmatian, of all things. Quite huge. Am not sure if you noticed. He was busy making a sort of dinosaur-hole on the beach when we all filed up to congratulate you, so you didn't shake his paw. I whisked off the plate and chair we had reserved for him and found him a big bowl of water instead. Ben watched me with curious eyes but refrained from comment, thank God.

I swallowed when I discovered that Spotty's Kerry is a stunning thirty-something whose ancestral lines must have touched Sitting Bull and Grace Kelly somewhere en route. I didn't know you had people like that in your family! Did you see her black masses of hair? That creamy skin color? Those large blue eyes?

But, not enough to bear, I also did myself a bad turn by putting John at the opposite end of the room. One detail I only noticed when we sat down, and by then it was too late to change anything about it.

He was in full view from my place. Every time I glanced up, I saw his profile, his bent head, as he listened to the dark beauty. I might add that he didn't even once waste a glimpse on me.

He looked magnificent in his tux and wore it with the ease of someone who doesn't feel like a penguin in such an outfit. Well, I guess with the life he leads, he's used to it.

He talked to Ben's grandmother too, and I heard his laugh when she told him some anecdote from her life. It pierced me.

As if our first encounter hadn't destroyed me already.

While you were approaching the lighthouse at a stately pace of 10 mph in your creamy vintage Mercedes, I raced ahead and stationed myself in front of the entrance. Trying to appear as if everything was under control, I handed out the tiny roses and helped to fix them on lapels.

Then John and Gerry came up.

Thank God for Gerry. He gave me a bear hug (followed by a doubting look at his father) and told me he had missed me. I blinked to suppress my tears and squeezed out some light reply. With blind eyes I fixed the rose at Gerry's lapel and told him he could choose his seat wherever he wanted. His mouth dropped when he realized the ceremony would be outside, with the ocean as backdrop. "Cool," he said. "Lucky it isn't raining."

"Yes, indeed. Isn't the weather perfect?" My voice wobbled as I tried to pretend we were having a normal conversation.

Gerry seemed to have grown (his shoes reminded me of small boats), and with two strides he catapulted himself out of earshot, securing the right seats.

I took a deep breath and faced John.

His gray eyes were like quartz again as he looked at me.

"Nice to see you," I mumbled (trust me to make scintillating conversation whenever it's needed!) and lifted the rose.

"Is it really?" he said. He took the rose from me and affixed it himself.

And then he turned on his heels and was gone before I could think of a reply. Any reply.

I hope the slight prick I inflicted on your Uncle Arthur won't get infected. You see, he came next, and my hands were still trembling.

I'll never forget the expression on Brad's face as he took your hand in the ceremony. Until then I had felt a bit uneasy about the whole thing; I admit it now. It all happened so fast, you know. But maybe sometimes, when you feel it's right, you shouldn't hesitate anymore and go right ahead, never mind principles and caution. I see that now.

I do, do, do hope you'll be happy ever after, Leslie.

I took a deep breath when the service ended. A wedding is so momentous, so dramatic, I always get into trouble with my breathing. But I knew that if I started to cry, I might not stop before seven the next night, so I made a superhuman effort and kept a stiff upper lip.

I had wondered if I couldn't corner John during the Champagne reception. It was such a perfect setting, and with the warm sun and the festive mood, I thought it might mellow him a bit. But I soon realized it was much too risky. For one, I couldn't simply drag him behind the lighthouse, and also, people kept coming up to me, asking tons of questions.

And then Ron presented Jenny to me.

I do know Jenny after all! And so do you! Did you recognize her? She's the eldest daughter of Mr. Barnes, whose land adjoins Rob's. It's a perfect match. She's only turned twenty (I felt like an owl next to her), but she thinks the sun rises and sets with Rob, and he so deserves someone like that after the hard times I put him through.

I'm afraid I threw myself onto her neck, staggering her (and myself), but I couldn't hold back. I'm so glad for him. He walks differently too. Sort of proud and self-assured.

When I came up again from the hug, I discovered John standing only two paces away, watching our bursting-with-harmony gathering with a puzzled expression in his gray eyes.

I could feel myself turning beet red. Of course, John must have recognized Rob immediately. Oh, God.

I gathered up my dress and galloped away like a giraffe in a panic, hiding behind Uncle Arthur.

Later I overheard Jenny saying to Rob that I seemed to be somewhat eccentric. Eccentric! Made me feel ancient. I could already hear the tour guide saying, "And sitting over there at the jetty is old Karen—she's a bit eccentric, if you know what I mean—but if you humor her, she's absolutely harmless." Gah.

Admit it, all of this is news to you! I told you we had a lot going on at your wedding that you failed to notice! Thank God you have me to fill in the blank spots.

I already told you about dinner. You can't imagine how relieved I was that the orange-mousse stage passed without incident. I had a few nightmares filled with possibilities. As predicted, Ben quietly tucked away three or four, sitting on his grandmother's lap and entertaining John with a story that must have been truly riveting, because John stopped eating and didn't even notice when Ben exchanged their bowls and calmly polished off John's mousse.

Did you practice the waltz with Brad while you were ill? It looked picture-perfect, and when you raised your face to him and smiled in a way I've never seen you smile before, Leslie, I broke down.

I looked away—straight into John's eyes, right across the dance floor. A mixture of anger and regret flared up in his, and suddenly an old saying popped into my head: "There are no words more terrible than these two: *Too late.*"

That did it.

I turned on my heels and ran out, right down to the rocks, hurtling across them as if I was haunted. When I heard the soothing murmur of the sea and smelled the salty tang, I got a bit calmer, but I still had to bite my right fist to choke back the tears.

Suddenly I heard John's voice from somewhere above me. "Karen."

I couldn't reply. I hadn't imagined our meeting to be like that. I had planned to be composed.

And calm.

I wanted to tell him I had been a fool and that I regretted it all, and how I wished it had been different. Something along those lines.

I wanted to be serene, not a sniffling wreck.

"Karen. May I come down?"

What could I say? I managed some assenting noise without turning around.

A stone crunched, and then he stopped right beside me.

I could smell his aftershave and felt his sleeve brushing my bare arm.

"I talked to your fiancé tonight."

I whipped around. "What? Who? I'm not engaged!" It was too dark to make out his face.

"He told me he was going to marry you because you had lost the real love of your life. And that you were very sad, the way people are if someone dies."

"I . . . I . . ."

His voice was level when he continued. "He also said it was your own fault and that you regretted it a lot, but that it can't be reversed anymore."

"Oh."

"Next, he added something I didn't really understand. About some stuffing coming out. And that your real love was like his crocodile. I'm not sure if I got it right, though, because at that point, his speech got a little indistinct due to an enormous spoonful of orange mousse."

I started to laugh and cry at the same time. "John, I'm so sorry. You were right, of course. I was scared to be happy. It was all my fault."

The moon showed for a minute before hiding again behind a sailing cloud. John searched my face and asked me about Rob. I explained about him, and he said, "When you threw yourself into his arms that night at your store, it felt as if someone had kicked me in the stomach."

"I . . . I can imagine. I'm sorry. I was in a bit of a state because of Leslie's decision to sell our store."

"Ah, yes."

He held his breath when I told him I had decided to sell my part too and that we would sign the paperwork after your return. (I didn't tell you earlier, but the condition for doubling the price was that I would get out too and that we would make a quick decision.)

I tried to sound nonchalant when I said I could always buy a share in another bookstore somewhere else.

He gripped my hands so hard, it hurt. "Like where?"

I trembled down to my shoes, but just as I opened my mouth to say "Seattle," John said, "Karen, there's one thing you have to know."

My stomach coiled. "Yes?"

"If you want me, you have to come to me all by yourself."

"Oh."

At that instant I knew I could trust him. He would never crush me. Oh, he would fight for the things he believed in, but he would not stampede me into the ground in the process. Yes, I know you told me so a hundred times, but I had never managed to believe it before.

I wanted to tell him about my feelings, wanted to say I loved him, but the words all got stuck in my throat. You didn't expect anything better from your non-flirting friend, did you?

Finally I managed to pull myself together. "I want . . . you, John. I want to be together with you, no matter where. I've missed you so much."

"Thank God. I thought you'd never say it." And with that, he bent forward, pulled me close to him, and kissed me, so tender and sweet, my heart felt like a feather all at once.

An eternity or five minutes later, I can't say which, he said without letting me go from the circle of his arms, "Karen?"

"Hmm?"

"Want an M&M?"

I chuckled. "Yes, please."

And you won't believe it, Leslie. He slid one hand inside his dinner jacket and came out with a small package of M&M's. I held out my hand, he passed me one, and I put it into my mouth.

But it had the wrong shape, and with surprise, I took it out again and stared at it. It was a ring. A simple broad band with inlaid sapphires all around. It sparkled in the moonlight.

"For a minute I was afraid you'd swallow it." I could hear the laugh in his voice.

"John." I choked.

"You once said you didn't want to be engaged to me, even in sham. I hope this is the right moment to ask you if maybe, just maybe, you've changed your mind?"

I admitted I had. Changed my mind. Completely and wholeheartedly, and I can't tell you how glad I am I didn't swallow my engagement ring. It seems John never thought it would get as far as my mouth. And how clever of him to have chosen one that wouldn't get snagged inside a glove.

But when my head stopped being in a whirl (not to mention any other parts of myself), I managed to ask why he had carried that ring here with him. It seemed incredible, after all I had put him through.

And he said, "Because I couldn't believe it was over. Contrary to you, my dear, I don't give up easily."

"In spite of thinking I had been two-timing you with Rob?"

He smiled a crooked smile there. And said that you, dear friend, told him he needn't worry about Rob. He stressed that that was all you said, in exactly those words, and not a single syllable more.

He said he was hurt and angry, but he wanted me to take the next step, because every time he tried to pull me closer, I turned and fled.

On thinking this over, I can't blame him, can I?

But as the days went by, and no word from me, he became rattled.

That's what he said.

Rattled.

I can't imagine John being rattled.

I told him your chicken pox was the only reason I didn't come to Seattle to have it all out. I also explained how I'd called Sandra, who'd lied to me on the phone.

At that point he frowned and asked me to repeat that conversation word by word. When I was done, he raised his eyebrows and told me that Sandra might just have stepped out of her office for a moment when he left his, and that was the reason she must have thought he was still in. Apparently he never changed his order that I should be put through immediately.

You know, Leslie, it never crossed my mind that there might be a perfectly legit explanation. We made a pact to stop wondering about hidden meanings and talk openly, always, in the future. I think it's a good way to remain sane.

You ask about Teton Valley? Of course I'll continue to teach skiing there. John said we might buy a place close to Candy's guesthouse, so he can always come and stay for a few days. He has gone through with the changes in his company and has started to take off every other Friday, so he'll come quite often. Doesn't that sound nice?

I still have to tell Candy we're engaged.

I'm engaged.

In the past, that sentence would have had me in cold sweat. Now it sounds wonderful, like an invisible bond between John and me, something precious just between us.

Well, there is one extra: I'll become a stepmother. So Gerry is definitely included too. He has already assured me he won't start calling me Mom. Phew. He has asked me, though, if the band can come to stay for another weekend when I'm in Seattle.

Will have to prepare John for it—and will have to make sure to be there.

See? I told you you missed quite a lot at your wedding.
Karen

Karen!!!

When I read your e-mail on my laptop, I jumped up and danced all over the bed. Snoodle shook his head and said, "Do you do this often? Someone should have told me about it before I agreed to marry you."

Hee-hee.

Here's to you and John, my friend—and to our NEW bookstore in Seattle!

Leslie

P.S. I believe a red-and-white-striped store awning would be just perfect for Seattle. Someone told me you would like it.